A Racecourse for Andy

by the same author

THE FEATHER STAR
DOWN TO EARTH

Patricia Wrightson

Illustrated by Margaret Horder

A Racecourse
for Andy

Harcourt, Brace & World, Inc. New York

Contents

1 Saturday Afternoon

Andy Hoddell stood on the pavement in Blunt Street and watched his friends taking turns on a skateboard. The street went plunging downhill into a deep hollow and rose steeply again beyond it. On this side of the street, the pavement ran down under high blank walls; on the opposite side, a row of quaint old cottages tipped downhill with the street. The cottages were clumsy and ugly, squashed together in terraces, and each had a tiny square of front garden. To make up for their sameness and their squat, narrow ugliness, they were all painted different colors: sooty blue, grimy green, pink fading to yellow, white turning gray. They all wore television antennae like crazy parasols on their roofs.

It was Saturday afternoon, and the crisscrossed, up-and-down streets of Appington Hill were very quiet. Still, the boys had to time their runs carefully, watching for the cars that came tipping suddenly out of side streets. Each in turn, the boys went swooping downhill like birds, the wheels of the skateboard singing on the asphalt. Near the bottom of the hill, Wattle Road cut across Blunt Street in a longer, easier slope to the left. Sometimes the skateboard would

swing away down this slope; sometimes it would plunge
straight on into the hollow, past the entrance to Beecham
Park Trotting Course, and mount a little way up the opposite rise. No one knew which it would do. Even the rider
hardly knew until he had started his run, with the wind in
his ears and the board vibrating under his feet, whether he
would lean a little to the right and resist the curve or lean
a little to the left and slip into it. Those at the top of the hill
would watch expectantly until the moment passed; and every time, whether the board turned and disappeared or went
straight on, Andy Hoddell would laugh excitedly. That was
his share of the game.

Mike and Terry O'Day owned the skateboard, having
made it from a bit of board and an old roller skate. They
stood together on the pavement and watched its performance critically—two stern, long-nosed faces, two pairs of
narrowed brown eyes, two heads of red-brown hair. Terry's head was a little lower than Mike's, for Terry was
eleven and Mike twelve.

"A bit too long in the back," said Terry. "I told you before."

"You're off your rocker," declared Mike.

"Half an inch too much behind the back wheels. She'll
tip up backwards one of these days."

"That'll be the day."

There was no heat in this argument, but Joe Mooney
knew it could go on, flat and unyielding, for hours. There
hadn't seemed to be anything wrong with the skateboard
when he was riding it, but he watched it anxiously on its
way down the hill. "Maybe she's a *shade* long in the back."

"She'll do," said Terry, changing sides at once to agree with Mike. The O'Day boys never allowed anyone else into their private arguments.

Andy, leaning against a brick wall that was scaly with dirt and age, had listened to the argument as he listened to all his friends' discussions. A frangipani tree leaning over the wall threw a patch of shade on the pavement, and a stray dog had crept into the shade at Andy's feet. He stirred its ginger hair with his toe, and the dog thumped the pavement with its stumpy tail.

Matt Pasan had finished his ride and was climbing the hill with the board tucked under his arm. The others watched him come slowly up, past the high blank walls and closed ticket windows of the trotting course, pausing to allow a car to pass before he crossed Wattle Road, then coming on up the steepest part of the rise. He was out of breath, and his hair clung to his damp forehead in the heat of early summer, but he shouted cheerfully in spite of it.

"Right to Ma Willock's gate—like to see you beat that."

"Like to see 'em beat that!" shouted Andy suddenly. "Eh, Matt?"

The others looked at him with the patience of long habit, neither forced nor polite. They were used to Andy and accepted him.

"Your turn this time, Andy," called Matt, teasing. "Come on, have a go!"

Andy laughed uneasily, waiting to see what they expected of him.

"Turn it up, Pasan!" called Joe quickly. "He's having you on, Andy. There's too many cars."

Andy laughed again, this time with relief. "You can't fool me, Matt Pasan!" he called. "I wouldn't ride that thing. It's too long in the back." He smiled warmly at all his friends and leaned back against the wall, out of their way.

Matt came up, his dark, lively face bent over the skateboard while he felt its wheels, testing their firmness. Joe watched seriously. His thin, long-jawed face was often serious. Joe was as tall as Mike O'Day, and the same age. Matt, like Terry, was a year younger. With their eyes fixed on the skateboard, none of them noticed a gray police van coast silently to the curb behind them. They jumped a little and stared at their feet when the constable's stern voice reached them.

"All right, you boys," said Constable Grace from the window of the van. "Get that board off the street. We've got enough accidents to worry about without you asking for more. Get going, now; and if I catch you again, I'll be having a word with your dads."

Reluctantly, the boys stirred. Terry muttered, "My go next time," and tucked the board under his arm. They trailed off slowly across the street toward the ugly little cottages. Only Andy stayed where he was and looked bewildered.

"What's up?" he called after them. "We aren't hurting, are we? What's up with *him?*" He frowned at Constable Grace and called again, "Joe! Where you going? You wasn't doing no harm!"

Joe paused in the middle of the street and waited. "Come on, Andy. We got to go."

A black storm came over Andy's face. He shouted at the constable. "They wasn't doing no harm!" His mouth seemed too small and slow to make the words come fast enough. "Matt—Terry—Joe—wasn't doing no harm! You're a big *urger*. That's what you are."

Joe and Mike had gone back and taken Andy's arms. "Put a sock in it, boy," they muttered urgently. "It's all right; we don't mind. Come on. It's *all right*, I tell you."

"Urger!" shouted Andy, craning back at the constable as he was led away. "Great big urger! *Urger!*" The constable waited passively. He had opened the door of the van and was ready to hold up any traffic that might suddenly appear in the narrow street.

"Will you *come on?*" said Mike, exasperated. "You'll end up getting the lot of us in bad with the cops."

"He's a great big urger, that's what he is," Andy explained indignantly. "You wasn't doing no harm."

"It's for our own good," Joe soothed him. "He doesn't want us getting knocked off by cars, that's all. We're going to have a look at the joss house now."

Andy frowned, muttered, and was silent. They hurried him around the nearest corner and out of the constable's sight. There Joe and Mike dropped Andy's arms and looked at each other, breathing deeply. Terry was frowning; he hated to be made to look foolish. Matt said, "Whew!" and suddenly exploded into chuckles.

"The big urger!" he gasped.

In a minute they were all giggling and looking at Andy with a sort of admiration. Andy's black scowl faded. He grinned, too, and began to swagger a little. When the others went on, he dropped contentedly behind them and followed. His eyes, which were round and very blue, were as placid as usual. His face, which was round, too, was as warm and friendly as usual. At the back of his head, where the crown was, his fair hair stuck up in little spikes that would never lie flat.

Andy was almost as tall as Mike and Joe, and a little

heavier. From the time the boys were very small, so long ago that even Joe and Mike could hardly remember, they had all played together in their narrow back yards and in the lanes and streets of Appington Hill. In those days they were all the same as each other, or as nearly the same as five different boys can be; and in those days Andy was the one everyone wanted to play with. It was Andy who invented the best games, who would always lend his ball or his bike, who was always so glad to see people that it was fun just to meet him. When there were fights, it was Mike or Terry who started them, Joe who fretted about them, Matt who was hurt and astonished by them, and Andy who patched them up. It was Joe who watched and worried over the two smaller boys but Andy who made them feel wanted in the game. In other ways Andy was the same as the other four. They all started school at nearly the same time. Then something happened. Somehow, little by little, a window seemed to close on Andy. Now he went to a separate school, and they all knew, even Andy himself, that he was different.

Andy lived behind a closed window. When he smiled his warm smile and spoke a little too loudly, it was as if he were speaking through the glass. When he listened carefully to what people said and paused for a second before he answered, it was as though their words came to him through the glass. Sometimes when he was with other people, his face wore a patient, waiting look as if he didn't know they were there. Sometimes he walked by himself with bright eyes and a ready smile, as if he didn't realize that the other people had gone. He had moments of noisy laughter or fierce anger when it seemed that he was knocking against the window. Even his face looked a little distorted, the way things sometimes look through glass. Still, because he was Andy, always warm and admiring, always glad to see them and careful not to be a nuisance, the others were still his friends.

Andy and Matt lived in the same row of squashed cottages, all joined together, with front doors opening straight onto the street. When they sat in their front rooms watching television, only a yard of space and a brick wall separated them from the people walking by on the pavement. Their street ran into the one where Joe lived in a house that stood by itself, squat and important. It had bulging front windows, and there were garlands of plaster fruits and flowers decorating its outer walls. Farther along this street there was a terrace of tall well-shaped cottages with grilles of delicate iron lace across their upper balconies. The O'Day boys lived in one of these. Their back yards, hidden behind high fences of palings or rusty corrugated iron, opened into a narrow lane. The boys turned into this lane so that Terry could push the skateboard through the O'Days' back gate. Then they went on, through steep streets and narrow lanes, toward the waterfront where the Chinese joss house was tucked away.

"Not worth it, really," Mike pointed out. "Even if you climb up the fence, what can you see? A couple of old houses, one dragon, and a lantern or two. We've seen all that. I'd rather poke about in the timber yards near the water."

"Do that too, why not?" said Joe. "It's not much further."

"I'll charge you to go in," said Matt with a grin. "I own the timber yards."

This was part of a game they had played continuously for a long time. Once it had been half serious; now it had become a habit.

"You do? I thought that was Terry's?"

"I bought it off him one day a couple of weeks back. Didn't I, Terry?"

"For a measly eight thousand," Terry grumbled. "I should've charged you more."

"Have you spent the eight thousand yet?" Mike asked him. "Sell you the Public Library for it."

"No. It's too far away—you hardly ever see it. I'll look around for a bit, I reckon."

"I own the Port Jackson Steamship Company," said Joe suddenly. He added, "That gives me all their ferries."

There was a respectful silence. No one had thought of claiming the steamship company before, though they "owned" all the most valuable parts of Sydney between them. The usual way to acquire property these days was to buy or swap for it from each other; but Joe had discovered a new claim and could take it up free. It was a good one, too.

"Swap you the timber yards for it," said Matt.

"Swap you the Town Hall," said Terry.

Joe smiled a little, pleased with his new property. "No, thanks. I reckon I'll stick to the ferries for a bit."

From behind came a hopeful voice. "I own Stebbins' shop. Matt! Hey, Mike! I own Stebbins' shop."

"You can't," Joe explained patiently over his shoulder. "Old Tom Stebbins owns that." Andy could never understand this game, however hard he tried. No one could make him see that you couldn't simply claim something that belonged to someone else. It had to be public property, or owned by so many people that you couldn't know who they were, so that they might as well not exist. You couldn't simply pinch his shop from old Tom Stebbins.

Andy tried again. "I own the police station!"

They broke into laughter, remembering Constable Grace.

"Good on you, Andy!"

"That's it, boy. You show 'em!"

"The police station—that'll come in handy!"

The lonely, shut-in look closed over Andy's face. He had lost contact with his friends again. At the next corner he slipped quietly away. It was some time before the others noticed, and when they did, they were not very surprised.

"Old Andy's faded out somewhere."

"Probably got hungry and went home."

By then, Andy was sitting on a small corner of vacant land above one of the plunging streets of Appington Hill. It was a place he often came to when he was alone. The ground was covered with rank grass, scraggy bushes, old cardboard cartons, and a scattering of tins and bottles. A great old Port Jackson fig tree hung over a fence behind it, making dark caves of shadow under its wide branches. A lane ran off from one corner. In the mouth of this lane and under bushes and deep in the shadows of the fig, green and yellow eyes blinked and widened where the brave, shabby stray cats were hiding. Andy had already sought out two or three and spoken a few words to them. They gave him evil looks, ears flattened and lips drawn into silent snarls;

but they stayed where they were. Andy thought it was friendly of them. He liked to look about and see them waiting and blinking in the shadows.

He sat on a rock in the late afternoon sun, muttering to himself and looking at the world. From here, the steep slopes of Appington Hill were like one-half of a broken basin with bare green parkland spilling out of the bottom and running away to the waterfront. Across its base were the walls of the trotting course, and behind them its grandstands rising at the edge of the park. Around the sides and rim of the basin crowded rows of old houses, clumsy, quaint, graceful, or stolid. To the right, not very far away, rose the tall buildings of the city of Sydney. Beyond the park and the upper reach of the harbor rose other ridges with other climbing streets and clustering houses. The roofs, towers, and chimneys of the skyline were softened by a haze that the late sun was turning to gold. Andy sat on his rock and looked at it all until he began to feel hungry. Then he wandered away down the lane to his own street.

Andy's mother was a dressmaker, and her work filled their small front room. There were paper patterns, tape measures, scissors, and pins on the big table. There were oddly shaped snippets of red, green, and gold material on the floor. Half-finished dresses and blouses hung on hangers against the wall. Mrs. Hoddell herself was in the kitchen cooking dinner. She was thin, fair, and very neat, and she looked at Andy with a bright smile that had something darker and more troubled behind it.

"Sausages!" said Andy, and laughed. He went to sit at the table, but his mother stopped him.

"You know better than that, love. You haven't washed

your hands, have you? I don't know what people must
think of you, getting in such a mess. Go and clean up
now."

Andy went down a narrow passage to the bathroom. It
had brick walls, a sloping ceiling, and a bath that stood on
four clawed feet. In the bottom of the bath a long strip of
black showed through the white enamel. Andy washed,
combed his hair, and went back to the table.

He ate his dinner carefully because his mother was
watching; but when she went to the stove to make the tea,
his hand crept quietly to his plate to gather up a few peas
and pop them in his mouth. When he had finished, he
frowned solemnly.

"That policeman's a great big urger," he told his mother.

She sat quite still for a second. "Policeman? Andrew
Hoddell, what have you been doing?"

"Wasn't doing no harm. Mike and Joe wasn't either. Just
riding their skateboard, that's all. He's a big urger."

Mrs. Hoddell relaxed and brushed the hair back from
her forehead. "Don't you go using words like that, or you'll
have your mouth washed out. The police are there to look
after you. A fine job they'd be doing, letting you get your-
selves knocked over and killed."

All at once an immense voice spoke across the roof tops
of Appington Hill. It was like a giant's voice, reaching
down into the room where they sat, full of authority. Mrs.
Hoddell gave it a moment's attention and glanced at the
clock on the mantelpiece. Andy shifted restlessly in his
chair. This was the voice that spoke from the amplifiers of
Beecham Park, intoning the approach of the first race.

Mrs. Hoddell stood up. "Nearly six—I'd better get busy. What are you doing this evening?"

"Going to Matt's," said Andy, pushing back his chair.

"Mind you stay with him, then. Don't get mixed up with any strangers. You never know who you'll run into on a race night."

Andy nodded wisely and went out to the front door.

2 *View from a Cliff*

It was still light when Andy stepped out on the pavement;
a glowing apricot light threw no shadows but washed the
ugly little houses with pink and lit their chimneys with gold.
The streets, which had been so quiet in the afternoon, were
full of the sound of cars. There were cars lining both sides
of the narrow street and the lanes that led from it, barely
leaving room between the rows for other cars to drive. A
man in a white dust coat patrolled the lines of cars in a solemn and watchful manner with his hands clasped behind his
back. The giant voice hung over the roofs and filled the
street, singing a chant composed of the names of horses.

Another car came nosing along the street, its worried
driver looking for a place to park. The man in the white
coat became active and commanding. His arms made com-
forting, beckoning sweeps; he led the way into the nearest
lane; he pointed to a certain spot, and like an experienced
conductor directing an orchestra of nervous beginners, his
waving arms coaxed the car into the narrowest possible
space. Andy watched respectfully, knowing that the driver
would pay twenty cents for this performance. Twenty

cents for every single car in this street and its lanes—how rich the man in the white coat must be!

The chanting voice had swept into a frenzy and died away. The first race was over. Andy went up the crooked street to Matt's place. The door from the pavement stood open for coolness, and just inside it Mr. and Mrs. Pasan were watching television. The white light from the screen flickered over them: Mrs. Pasan with her black hair drawn tightly back from her thin bird's face; Mr. Pasan sprawled heavily in a large chair, his shirt open in front and his feet stretched out in red and black socks. An unnaturally large face on the screen spoke to them in a friendly and confiding way about the Common Market.

"Lotta bull," said Mr. Pasan. "They'll do what they gotta do. You looking for Matt, Andy? He's out."

"He's round at O'Days'," added Mrs. Pasan.

Andy stood on the pavement for a moment, admiring Mr. Pasan's socks and his air of large relaxation. Then he went loping away in the pink and golden light.

The street where the O'Day boys lived was lined with cars like all the others, and another white-coated man watched over them. Andy went beyond the street to the lane behind. Being unusually narrow and dark, with high back fences looming above it, there were only a few cars in it yet. Far down in the darkness Andy could see the light of a torch, as he had expected. He knew what the O'Day boys would be doing just now. Sure enough, their double gate was open, and Terry and Matt stood by it with the torch. There were six cars parked in the paved yard, and there was space for only one more. The back door was also open, and the long, lean form of Mr. O'Day lounged in the doorway against the light. Mike and Joe were inside the gate, waiting for a seventh car to fill the yard.

"Lot of Sunday drivers," Mr. O'Day was grumbling. "There's room for nine or ten if they knew how to park a car. Who's that?"

"Andy Hoddell."

"You get out of the way behind that utility, Andy."

Andy slipped into the safe corner that Mike showed him and waited. The enticing of cars into the O'Days' back yard on race nights was to him a business venture as important and exciting as anything that went on in the city. Headlights crept into the lane, and Terry began to beckon with a torch. The car approached, turned in, and was directed by Mike to its place under the rotary clothesline. As the driver dimmed his lights and as Mr. O'Day came down toward him, Mike muttered, "That's the lot. Let's go." Terry pushed the flashlight into his father's hand; they went out to the lane.

The apricot light had faded into dusk. Pavements had become narrow alleys between front fences and lines of parked cars. In Blunt Street, where the skateboard had gone dipping and singing in the quiet afternoon, the gates and ticket windows of Beecham Park were open, and people came and went in little groups. Bus after bus turned into Wattle Road. A horse float came slowly down the hill. The tops of the grandstands, where they showed above the wall, were edged with golden drops of light from strings of electric bulbs. The wordless hum of many voices was drowned by the voice from the amplifiers. Beginning with calm authority, it passed into a chant, mounted to a frenzy, and was drowned in the roaring of a crowd.

"Looks like a big night," said Joe knowledgeably. They wandered to two or three points from which they might see into the course, but as usual every place was filled by silent groups of men. Most of the groups had large paper bags filled with bottles.

"The kids that sell programs make a bit of cash," said Matt with envy. "I'd have a go, but my old man goes mad about it."

"What do you want cash for?" said Mike. "You've got enough for a bag of chips."

They turned away from Beecham Park and went up the hill toward Ma Eaton's dim little corner shop.

Set in a row of dark cottages, the windows of the little shop glowed softly. Even inside, it was only dimly lit. Ma Eaton, short and stout, leaned on the counter and watched the street with sharp interest. She gave the boys her smile that was too wide and too sweet and supplied five packets of potato chips. The boys carried them around the corner to the little room behind the shop. Here Ma Eaton had installed a jukebox and three pinball machines. She said it was to give the young people somewhere to go and to keep them off the streets.

"You can't expect them to sit home with us old fogies," she would say, smiling too widely. "And what else is there but mischief? They're all right in my little room. There's nothing nasty like poker machines of course—no prizes or any of that—just real games of skill." And her cash register clanged busily as she changed their pocket money into coins to use in the machines.

The older girls and boys did make a sort of club room of Ma Eaton's tiny back room. Those of Joe's and Mike's

age could rarely fit inside it, but they stood about on the
pavement outside to listen to the jukebox and observe their
elders. Charlie and Greg Willis were there now, lingering
watchfully outside the narrow door. Inside, an unshaded
globe threw a yellow light over the room. Rhondah Blessing and Lexie Harris were bending over the "Whirlwind"
machine where little lights were flashing on and off—
red, yellow, blue, and green. Rob Regent was hopefully
feeding a leather belt into the "Jungle" machine, while the
two older Perkins boys looked on. The group on the pavement watched with interest, but the belt didn't seem to be
having any effect.

Andy hung back in the shadows. Charlie and Greg Willis
were not friends of his. They had a bouncing, confident way
that he distrusted.

"Saw you riding down Blunt Street," Greg was saying to
Mike. "You want a board that *is* a board. Let you have a go
on one of ours tomorrow if you like."

"No thanks," said Mike stiffly. "Ours'll do us."

"Not bad for a homemade board, I'll give you that. Just
a bit long in the back. She'll tip up backwards one of these
days."

Terry curled his lip like a dog. "*You* wouldn't know,
Willis. The only board *you'll* ever have is one out of a
shop."

Matt chuckled. Joe grinned slowly. Andy wandered off
into the dark. The giant voice from Beecham Park began
to intone another race. Andy thought he would go to the
next corner and look at the white-coated man in the street
beyond.

He reached the corner and saw the gleam of cars under dim street lights. The white coat of the attendant was a ghostly shape far down the street. There was a lot of cheerful noise from one of the houses where a party was going on, and Andy went down to listen. He stood outside the house for some time, laughing in the darkness at the gaiety inside.

Suddenly, a voice shouted at him. "You! What are you hanging around for?" The white-coated man was coming back, calling to him. Andy was startled. He slipped across the street and into a dark little passage between two rows of houses.

He stumbled over stones and rubbish, feeling along the wall of one house. He had been this way once or twice by daylight but never at night. It was quite black in the passage, but he felt his way toward a grayness at the other end until he came out in a place he scarcely remembered.

There was rough grass under his feet and in front a wide darkness scattered with distant lights. Behind him was the row of little cottages with front doors to which no caller ever came and front gates opening on no street or pavement. Only a strip of rough, grassy ground, with outcrops of sandstone, lay in front of the houses, and beyond this the curving edge of a cliff. Andy could see, twenty or thirty feet below, the windy, lamp-hung treetops and green stretches of the park leading away to the docks and the far lights of the city. A wire mesh fence guarded the edge of the cliff at this end; but farther along, where the cliff curved back, there was no fence. He turned that way, stumbling over rough ground in the dark. There was noise and light

and movement down there, where the grandstands of
Beecham Park Trotting Course rose between this cliff and
a matching one beyond them. Andy reached the edge of
the cliff and looked down into the circle of high walls and
buildings, into the glowing, lively magic of Beecham Park
on a race night.

There were the great stands edged with strings of lights,
and the white oval of the rails, with the brown oval of the
track lying inside it. A restless crowd of people drifted before the stands and washed along the rails. There were huge
boards where red lights flashed and numbers rose and fell.
Over the track hung a ring of floodlights, spraying misty
showers of light; and a band in dark uniforms marched on
the track, playing music that made Andy laugh. Within the
track was a pool of shadows rippling with the gleam of
parked cars. Outside it, where the crowds were drifting,
there was a crop of little red-topped stands where bookmakers were giving their short, sharp cries. Outside the circling walls of the course, rows of buses and crowds of
parked cars spread away into streets and parkland.

Behind Andy, on the row of little dark verandas, there
was sometimes a stir or a murmuring voice. Other people,
who belonged here, were watching the lively magic of race
night. To be away from them, Andy climbed over the edge
of the cliff to a shelf of sandstone two or three feet down.
He sat there, poised above the light and color of Beecham
Park.

The band marched away, and the voice from the amplifiers began to intone. It no longer sounded like the voice of
a giant speaking from the rooftops. Here it was in propor-

tion to all the rest, the right sort of voice to speak from the lighted stage of the racecourse. The crowd flowed into the stands or was washed into a line along the rails. The book-makers' cries stuttered loudly like firecrackers, then fell silent. Everything was silent except the voice singing its chant of names. There came a whispering along the track and a soft beating like silken drums. The horses swept by in a dark, shining mass drawn out along the rails. The wheels of their gigs whirled and whispered; the drivers' silks shone like jewels, scarlet, sapphire, gold, and green; the horses lifted their proud cockaded heads; their legs shone and flashed to the soft thudding of drums. Whips beat, and the whole mass vanished behind a stand. The voice sang on: *Magic Circle . . . Falling Star . . . Southern Rose . . . Sunfire . . .* Again the horses flashed and passed. A third time they came, and this time a great, roaring crowd-voice traveled around the course with them. The chanting rose to a frenzy; lights flashed; the mass of horses broke into scattered flying units. The race was over.

Andy leaned back against the wall of the cliff. He was too breathless to chuckle or mutter. The light from the racecourse threw a pale gleam over his face: his eyes staring, full of warmth and wonder, his mouth open, spikes of hair sticking up on the back of his head. Hardly knowing where he was, he sat on his high perch and watched for a long time.

After a while he began to feel cold and stiff. His head was dazed with color and movement, but the stone of the cliff was hard and cold. He climbed up stiffly, stumbled through the darkness until he found the narrow passage by which he had come, and went home. There was still a coming and going of cars in the streets, and the white coats of the attendants glimmered under the street lights; but Andy passed them without seeing. His mother was still working in their front room, and she had the kitchen clock on the table where she could see it.

"You've been a long time," she said, putting her work away while the lines smoothed out of her face. "What have you all been up to? Concocting some wonderful thing in O'Days' toolshed, I suppose."

Full of secrets and splendor, Andy smiled at her dimly and went to bed.

He woke up early, while Mrs. Hoddell was still asleep. The secrets and splendor were still there. He wanted to go back to the cliff and look down by daylight; but he knew it was Sunday, and he was supposed to go to church. He dressed, worrying about his mother and whether she could be late for church because of waiting for him. He decided to leave her a message. He found a pencil and paper, wrote "Gone," and left this message on the kitchen table. Then he took a banana and a piece of cake and went out by the front door.

The street was empty and very quiet. A small girl in pajamas sat in one of the doorways and pushed her doll's carriage backward and forward across the pavement. An old woman, shapeless in a cotton gown, with a long braid of gray hair swinging over her shoulder, opened another door and took in a bottle of milk. Andy loped past with the long, bouncing stride he used when he wanted to get somewhere quickly. He made his way through the quiet streets till he reached the row of back gates that belonged to the cliff-top houses. He slipped through the little passage and came out on the jutting rocks and rank grass near the cliff.

A man was sitting in the sun on the front steps of one of the cottages, reading a Sunday paper. Andy went quietly down to the farther end of the cliff and climbed over as he had last night.

There was the racecourse, empty and still inside its high walls. The stands were gaunt and colorless in the morning sun. Newspapers and racing programs littered the ground outside the rails and lay in drifts along the walls. Only the broad green oval inside the track had any life or color. The rest looked bare, ugly, and self-important.

Andy was delighted with it. "You wouldn't know," he said with a chuckle. "If you didn't see it, you wouldn't know." So cunningly, by daylight, did the racecourse hide the shifting, glowing magic that had filled it the night before. Beyond its walls the empty parklands stretched away to the docks, far more pleasant to look at. There were trees there, and the winding storm-water channel where a glint of water reflected the sky. There were the deep and shady arches on which the railway swept across in a wide curve. To look at it, anyone would think that the open park was a pleasanter, more interesting place than the racecourse. Andy laughed.

As he brooded over it, he saw that there was, in fact, some movement inside the high walls of the course. A single horse was running on the track, drawing its gig easily and swiftly behind. It wore no cockade, and its driver had only drab overalls. Close to the high wall on the nearer side, Andy could sometimes glimpse a movement of men who seemed to be sweeping. He began to scramble down and along the rocks, sliding and bumping to the bottom of the cliff.

He reached the bottom and stood in the lower part of Wattle Road, where buses had been standing in long rows last night. Across the road was the southern wall of

Beecham Park, with a litter of paper strewn along it. Andy crossed the road and walked along under the wall. There seemed to be no way in. At the corner he turned into Blunt Street and went steeply downhill, following the eastern wall. All the gates, roller doors, and ticket windows were closed. Not till he reached the lowest and farthest corner did he find a high gate of wire mesh that stood open.

Andy stood shyly in the gateway and looked across the broad grounds.

3 The Man with the Bottles

The men with brooms were now far away on the other side of the course. Andy was standing at one end of the big stand that he had seen filled with people last night. There was a beating of hoofs, a shirring of wheels, and the horse swept by behind the rails. He had a glimpse of its deep chest and powerful legs and the concentrated frown of the driver. When it had passed, he looked again at the grandstands, the clutter of smaller buildings, the grounds lying green and quiet in the sunlight, and up at the cliffs that stood over it on two sides with little remote houses clinging to their tops. He stood there, just inside the gateway, with his hair sticking up in spikes and his round blue eyes full of warmth and admiration for Beecham Park Trotting Course.

He was just looking at the big stand when an old bent man came toward him from that direction, carrying a sack on his back and peering about as he came. For a moment Andy wondered if the old man would send him away, but the faded green trousers and baggy gray jacket that he wore looked homely and not frightening. Andy gave his warm and friendly smile. The old man peered at him with faded blue eyes and nodded. Then he lowered the sack, picked up an empty bottle from the ground, and put it in the sack. There was a clanking of many bottles as he hefted the sack to his shoulder again and came on.

"Do they let you in there?" Andy asked admiringly.

The old man wobbled a white mustache that was stained with yellow. His face had deep downward creases and a lot of gray stubble on the chin. "Like to see 'em keep me out," he boasted huskily. "They'll set the dogs on *you* if they catch you inside."

"I'm not doing no harm," said Andy, who had no fear of dogs. The old man prodded at a pile of newspapers, looking for more bottles. "It's good here," said Andy dreamily, looking at the sheltering walls. "It's the best place I know."

> *I own the timber yard!*
> *I own the Town Hall!*
> *I own the ferries!*

"I wish I owned this place," said Andy. "Don't you wish you owned this place, mister?"

The old man stared fixedly. The lines on his face set deeper, and some sort of spark lit in his faded eyes. "Nothing but a packet of trouble, this place. Sell it to you cheap if you like." He came closer, till he was stooping forward right into Andy's face. His own was patterned with little red veins and patches of gray skin. "Three of these newfangled dollars, *there's* a bargain for you. I been wanting to get rid of it. It's too much for me, or I wouldn't let it go so cheap. Come on now, what do you say? You won't do better, I'm telling you. Three dollars, take it or leave it."

Andy stared at him and laughed and laughed. The spark in the old man's eyes twinkled back. "I never knew it was yours!" cried Andy, laughing again. "You know what, mister? I never knew it was your place!"

"Three dollars," repeated the old man, "and that's my last word. Don't waste my time if you haven't got it."

"I don't know if I got it or not," said Andy, chuckling excitedly. "I got some in my money box, but I don't know if it's three dollars."

"I won't be beaten down on my price," said the old man, grimly playful. "Three dollars, and a bargain at that." He shifted the sack on his shoulder and walked off, clanking.

Andy ran after him a little way. "I bet I got three dollars, mister!" he called. "You wait and see!" But the old man disappeared into the back door of a hotel across the street. Andy started for home at once to open his money box.

He knew he was not supposed to do this. His mother looked after his money box for him and put something in it whenever he delivered a parcel of sewing for her. Andy himself put in odd coins from time to time, whenever he had one to spare. He couldn't remember that it had ever been opened, except once when he put some buttons in for a joke. His mother had needed the buttons. She had scolded him and had taken out a screw that held the two halves of the box together. There had been some money in the box then, and he thought that was a long time ago. He remembered with pleasure that he had learned to count money quite well.

"It's my money, anyhow," muttered Andy. His head felt as though a swarm of bees was buzzing about inside it. He had no thought to spare for the slow and stumbling way his feet were taking him through the crisscross, up-and-down streets.

A surly white terrier nosed at his heels. He clicked his

fingers at it from habit; the terrier's tail moved in salute,
and it trotted after him. Another, older and even more evil-
looking, joined the first. Then a bow-legged dachshund
and a foolishly grinning pup tumbled out of a lane, sniffed
him, and went running ahead. Andy climbed some steps
to the vacant lot where he sometimes sat and looked at the
city and crossed to the corner where the lane led out toward
his own street. The dogs paused and sniffed exploringly.
The terriers growled. The dachshund gave a deep bark. The
puppy set up a noisy yapping. Yellow eyes widened in the
shadows, fur stiffened, and lips snarled. Cats spat and hurtled over fences; dogs leaped and yelped. Andy stood still
in the lane and laughed with shock.

"I forgot!" he shouted to the fleeing cats. Then he fled
himself, down the lane. "Poor old cats," he muttered as he
ran. "They got stirred up, all right."

Mrs. Hoddell had gone to church, and the house was
locked. Andy climbed in through the bathroom window
and found his money box on the mantelpiece. He loosened
the screw with the blade of a knife and opened the box. A
little heap of silver fell out on the table. Andy sorted the
coins into separate heaps to make counting easier before he
began, with great care, to put them together into dollars.
There were two dollars, and a few coins left over. He
screwed the money box together again and then, because
the odd coins seemed somehow to be a nuisance, dropped
them back in through the slot. He found an empty pin box
on his mother's worktable to hold the two dollars, tucked it
under the mattress of his bed, and climbed out of the window again.

"That's all I got, only two dollars," he muttered. "I got to get another one yet." He wandered out to the street, thinking about it in a hopeful and determined way. "A dollar . . . a dollar, now. He said three of 'em, and there's only two. I gotta get another one somewhere."

Farther down the street he saw Matt and Joe strolling toward O'Days' place. He shouted and broke into his loping run to catch up with them.

"Here's old Andy," said Matt over his shoulder. "Going to have a go on the board today, boy?"

"I can't," said Andy, swaggering. "Got no time for that. I gotta find a dollar somewhere. Just thought I'd tell you."

Matt whistled, pretending to be impressed. "A dollar, eh? That's a lot of dough. What do you want it for?"

Andy screwed his round face into a look of great cunning and secrecy. "You'll see. Just wait, and then you'll see. I got two already, but there'll be another one yet."

Joe was looking at him thoughtfully. "Come on, Andy. You can tell us. What do you need three dollars for?"

Andy smiled his warm smile. "Don't you worry," he said kindly. "I'll get hold of him somewhere—you'll see. I just thought I'd tell you." He nodded, waved, and strolled off, leaving the others to stare after him. Joe was frowning a little, but Matt's lively face was alight with curiosity.

Andy didn't notice, for he was already thinking deeply about his problem. He thought about it all the morning and while he ate his lunch. His mother spoke kindly but seriously about his missing church and her disappointment at having to go alone. He listened for a little, and it made him feel very uncomfortable and sorry; so he let his face go on looking sad while his mind went back to thinking about the dollar. In the afternoon he went looking for empty bottles, exploring the park and storm-water channel as well as a number of garbage cans; but there were not many bottles of the right sort, and he raised only ten cents. After that he did some more thinking.

It took him five afternoons to raise the dollar. He tried knocking at the doors of people he knew and offering to run messages or mow lawns; but most of those who accepted his offer did so in a spirit of gratitude that made him too uncomfortable to ask for money.

"You're a real kind boy, Andy," said Ma Eaton, giving him a sweet smile and a spotty banana from the window of the shop. "I'll be sure and tell your mother what a help you've been. She ought to be real proud."

Andy gave up this scheme after two days, having raised only another twenty cents. He was wandering homeward down a lane, depressed and lonely, when he was startled by voices as shrill as the cry of a peewee.

"Look out, Andy Hoddell! . . . Watch what you're doing! . . . Why don't you look where you're going?"

Andy looked. One of his feet was planted on a square of green taffeta and the other poised above a circle of white velvet. These and other scraps of gay materials were laid out on a sheet of paper outside an open gate, where Irene Willis and Noela Black sat with scissors and reels of cotton. Two small dolls of very grown-up shape, with hard, shiny smiles and astonishing masses of silky hair, lay on their backs and stared glassily.

Andy stood still while he took all this in, then backed

slowly and awkwardly. "I never meant it," he said, feeling very bad. "I never saw. Is it all right?"

Irene was shaking and blowing the green taffeta. Both girls bent over it and muttered together. Neither of them answered him, but Andy was lost in thought. After a while he called to them, "Hey!"

They looked up in a hostile way.

"Do you want a lot more of that stuff?" said Andy, looking at the scraps of material. "I'll get you a whole lot more if you want it. Only twenty cents. All different colors."

They conferred. "I haven't got twenty cents," said Irene.

"What have you got, then?"

"Only ten cents."

"I'll get you some for ten cents if you want it. You could have had a whole lot for twenty cents, but I reckon you'll get a good bit for ten cents, if that's all you've got."

The two girls looked at each other. "His mother's a dressmaker," they said, nodding wisely.

"I've got ten cents, too," said Noela.

"I'll get two lots," said Andy. "You can go and find the money." He went loping home to find the bag into which his mother stuffed the small useless pieces of stuff that tumbled on the floor when she was cutting out. He dumped handfuls of gay scraps on two sheets of newspaper, and when he took the fat parcels back, each of the girls produced ten cents.

This was the most successful of Andy's efforts to earn money, and he still had only fifty cents. Since he could think of no more business deals, he resorted to an older and simpler method. He wandered into streets farther from home

and asked strangers for money, making use of his own odd-
ness and the effect it had on people.

A baby that hasn't yet learned to sit up knows a good
deal about the people around it—whether to cry for attention or play quietly in its cot. So Andy, living behind a
closed window, had learned to read faces through the glass.
He knew that some people, children and adults, would
rather not see him or talk to him. The children showed it by
running away or by teasing him until he himself was
hurt and angry enough to run away. The adults showed it
in the impatient way they spoke or by looking away quickly
and pretending not to see him at all. Some people found him
amusing at times when he was really quite serious, and he
would quickly pretend that he meant to be funny, to hide
his puzzlement. Other people treated him with a heavy
kindness that made him just as uncomfortable—but he knew
how to make use of it, too. Most people were a little more
patient and polite to Andy than they were to other boys.
He liked that best.

So now he went walking in the busier streets near the
traffic lights. He smiled at people and talked to them whenever he had the chance. If they answered in a cheerful and
friendly way or if they were carefully kind, he asked for
money "to buy a drink because I'm thirsty." In two afternoons he had collected fifty cents, enough to make up his
third dollar. It was by far the easiest way he had tried.

He put all his money in the pin box, fastened it with a
rubber band, and went out to look for the old man with the
bottles. It was late afternoon. The sun was no longer pouring heat down into the streets, but the streets themselves

threw back a wave of warmth. Andy, loping down Blunt Street, suddenly found the two O'Day boys standing in his way.

"And where have *you* been all the week?" demanded Mike a little sternly. "Have you been dodging us or what?"

Terry added, "Aren't we mates any more?" He and Mike were both curious, having heard from Joe and Matt that old Andy had some scheme for which he needed money.

Andy, brought to a sudden stop, chuckled and shifted his feet. He was pleased to see his friends and glad that they had missed him; but he could see the walls of Beecham Park, and he had the money, and the bees were buzzing in his head. "Can't wait," he said, dodging past. Over his shoulder he called, "See you one of these days," and went loping on his way.

He found the bottom gate of the racecourse standing open, but there was no sign of the old man. A car was parked in the center of the grounds, and a water cart drove slowly around the track, watering it. Andy stood in the gateway waiting for the old man, watching the jets of water spraying onto the track, admiring the big empty grandstand and the sheltered quiet inside the circling walls. He could hardly believe that soon it would all be his.

He watched until the water cart drove off, until a man came and locked the gate and the car drove off to the other side of the course. He waited until it was dark, but the old man didn't come. Andy went home. The next afternoon he waited again. It never occurred to him to look for the old man anywhere else, and he would have had no idea where else to look. He waited until the western skyline made a pattern of black blocks against the fading gold of the sky. Then, just as he was turning to go home, he saw a pair of old green trousers and a baggy gray jacket come lurching out of the hotel across the street.

It was the same old man. He went slowly and unsteadily up the hill, and Andy followed. Sometimes he came quite close and then dropped shyly back again. The old man turned into a narrow angled lane, and Andy was afraid of losing him. Then he hurried and caught up.

"Mister!" he called. "Hey, mister, I brought the three dollars."

The old man looked behind, swayed slightly, and walked on. Andy grabbed at his sleeve.

"I got 'em all, those dollars you said. You didn't forget, did you? It was hard work getting them."

The old man had stopped, turned, and was peering at Andy in a dull, unrecognizing way. His eyes were rather bloodshot.

"You gotta take the three dollars, mister," said Andy urgently. "You said cheap at the price because it's a packet of trouble. Don't you want 'em?" He was opening the pin box, which chinked as he took off the rubber band.

"Three dollars," said the old man in a hazy way. Then, to Andy's relief, he seemed to wake up a little. "You got three dollars for an old bloke? You're a good boy, a fine, big, strapping boy. Give it here." He held out his hand. Andy poured the silver coins into it. The old man poked them with an exploring finger.

"It's all there," said Andy.

"I thank you, my boy. . . . I was in the war, you know.

The real war, nineteen-eighteen. . . . The holy saints'll make it up to you, boy."

"Can I have it now?" said Andy.

The old man closed his fist tightly. "You just *give* it to me."

Andy laughed and laughed. "That's the money I gave you," he pointed out, still laughing. "I don't want the money, I want the racecourse. Is it mine now, mister? Can I have Beecham Park?"

"If you say so," said the old man. He waved his free hand in a broad and generous gesture. "Lock—stock—and barrel, boy. All yours."

Andy breathed deeply and laughed again with delight.

4 *The Practical Side*

Andy wandered slowly home in the twilight, chuckling now and then and muttering to himself. He had raised the money and paid the price; now Beecham Park Trotting Course was his. The first stars were glinting in the blue-black depths of sky, and he could not tell whether they were in the sky or in his head. The hard asphalt under his feet and the cottages squatting in dim rows on either side were not so real or so close as the quietness and splendor of his race-course. He thought how surprised his mother would be—then chuckled uneasily when he remembered his empty money box. He thought, instead, how surprised his friends would be. He wanted to go and tell them at once; yet in another way he didn't want to tell anyone at all. It was so big, his secret. He felt lost in it.

He was very quiet during the evening and went to bed even before Mrs. Hoddell had time to suggest it. Early in the morning he went out and looked at his racecourse. He saw three horses running with their gigs through a silvery, silken mist that lay over the grounds. In the afternoon he looked again and saw a yellow tractor raking the track level. He was still watching when he saw his four friends going by toward the open park behind the racecourse. Andy loped quickly after them, but then, when he caught up with them, he dropped back again with a new sort of shyness.

Matt nudged Terry, who was nearest to him. "See who's coming after us?" Terry, Mike, and Joe looked quickly back and went on walking. They were a little offended with Andy, who had kept away for a whole week, busy on some mysterious project that he had failed to explain. They went on in silence to the storm-water channel, where they hoped to find some useful pieces of timber to make a set of bails and stumps for cricket.

Among the rubbish that came washing down the storm-water channel, there were often things worth rescuing: bolts, bits of wire or rope, useful tins, or odd lengths of timber. The boys climbed down the cemented sides of the channel into its broad, gently curving bed, which was almost dry except for a trickle of water along its center. They began to work their way along it, pausing now and then to examine something, lifting aside a sheet of gray and brittle cardboard, rolling an empty bottle into the stream; conscious of Andy, who kept pace with them on the bank above and watched. Where the big willows hung over the channel, they found three or four pieces of timber that they threw out on the bank. Andy placed them in a neat stack while the others climbed out.

"What you want them for?" he asked.

"Making a wicket," said Joe.

Andy chuckled in a pleased and interested way. "Why don't you make another skateboard so's two could go at the one time?"

"No wheels," said Mike, climbing into one of the wil-

lows. Soon they were all sitting like birds among the
branches, while Andy sat contentedly under the tree.

"I own the dock yards," said Matt hopefully, looking
over the park toward them from his perch.

"*No*, you don't," said Mike firmly. "I've had them for months."

"I thought you might, but I wasn't sure. Just thought I'd have a go. Who's got Pyrmont Bridge?"

"Me," said Terry.

"What are you going to do with it?"

"Make a toll bridge of it. A bob to go over."

"All the traffic'll go through Railway Square for nothing. Who wants to pay a bob to go over Pyrmont Bridge?"

"Don't be a lunatic. There's enough traffic jams now when they *do* use Pyrmont. They'll pay."

The willow dipped and swayed as the boys moved from branch to branch. At the foot of the tree, Andy laughed with secret glee. "I own something, too!" he shouted into the branches.

There was only silence from above. They were not going to show an undignified curiosity about Andy's doings.

"Hey, Mike! Did you hear, Joe? I own something, too! Not just kidding like you do, though." He chuckled knowingly. "You don't really own all that stuff. *I* know. You never paid for any of it. What I own, I bought it."

"All right," said Joe. "We heard you the first time. *What* do you own?"

Andy screwed up his eyes and twisted his face cunningly.

"You needn't tell us if you don't want to," said Terry cruelly. "Nobody said you *had* to be friends."

"I'm friends!" cried Andy, deeply hurt. "Gee, you know I'm *best* friends. I'm going to tell you, aren't I? It's just . . ." His voice trailed off.

"Go on, Andy—good old Andy!" cried Matt, almost

bursting under the strain. "Spit it out, boy. Did you buy it with the three dollars?"

Andy tried to tell them, but the words seemed to be too big for his tongue to manage. "I'll *show* you," he said at last. "I'll show you tonight."

"I bet," said Mike, not believing him.

"You wait and you'll see," Andy promised, hugging himself.

He was very quiet for the rest of the afternoon, but now his friends saw that his quietness had a waiting, explosive quality like a bomb. Mike and Joe exchanged looks but said nothing. Matt was amused and made teasing remarks about "the big secret" until Terry told him briefly to stow it. There was a feeling of tension building up, and Joe's long quiet face grew more and more serious. Whatever it was that gripped Andy so that everything else was shut out, he had been wrapped up in it for a whole week. What could he have bought for three dollars that could keep him in this state of round-eyed, hushed excitement? It was too much money for Andy or it was not enough.

"He's bought a dog," whispered Matt.

Mike and Joe exchanged a thoughtful look. That was one thing Andy really might have done, about which he might be very excited.

"If he has, he's been rooked," muttered Terry. "The sort of mongrel he could get for three dollars, he could've picked up for nothing."

Mike was shaking his head. "No. If it was a dog, he'd tell us."

Evening came, and pale lights swung between treetops

in the park. The boys went home through streets that were roaring and humming with the sound of cars and where white-coated men had sprung up like a crop of Saturday-night mushrooms. Later, when the giant voice was speaking with calm authority into every ear in Appington Hill, Andy arrived in the O'Days' back yard before it was half filled and drove everyone frantic with his impatience.

"They're too slow tonight, aren't they, Mike? You won't wait for 'em if they don't come soon, will you? Don't you wish they'd hurry up, Terry? This is nearly enough now, isn't it?"

"Stand in that corner," said Mike, exasperated, "and don't move or *talk*."

At last the yard was filled. "Coming, Terry? You coming, Joe? Hey, Matt!" For once, Andy's friends followed him, and he swelled with pride and mystery as he led them, with many quiet chuckles, through the darkening streets. Halfway along the little passage, he stopped suddenly, made shy by the very importance of his secret. "You're my friends," he reminded them. "That's why I'm showing you."

"Get on with it then," said Mike unsympathetically.

They groped their way out to the cliff top, and Andy felt the presence of shadowy forms on verandas. "Sh-sh," he whispered mysteriously, and led the way down the rocks.

None of the others had the least idea of what was coming. When Andy said "There!" and threw out a hand to the wide circle of brilliance and movement below, they stared in a puzzled way. Andy sat on a rock shelf and chuckled in the dark. "That's it," he said at last, peering at them. Reflected light from below washed faintly over their faces. He could see that they were still mystified. "It's mine," he explained. "I bought it." He stood up suddenly and leaned forward in the night, clinging with his hands to the cliff face. "I own Beecham Park!" cried Andy triumphantly.

The other boys were completely silent. Andy chuckled and gazed and chuckled again. On the splendid stage below, the crowd drifted and swirled; the bookmakers shouted; the band marched and played.

"Three dollars and cheap at the price," said Andy. "I only got two in my box. I had to get another one." He was talking dreamily, half to himself. "It took a time. Mum doesn't know I opened the money box. . . . Don't you wish it was yours?" He looked at the shocked faces of his friends. "You can come and look at it any time," he assured them. "It's just the same as if it was yours."

Still they were silent, unable to realize that Andy had bought Beecham Park Trotting Course for himself. The tide of people flowed away; the bookmakers sputtered; the great voice spoke out.

"The horses!" cried Andy, his eyes wide in the pale reflected light. "They're coming! Can't you hear their feet, Joe?"

The dark, shining horses whirled their jeweled drivers around under the floodlights. Andy watched them, his face alight with pride and love. This was his, this bright circle in the dark night. He had bought it for three dollars.

Around him on the cliff, his friends stirred uneasily. Matt muttered, "Cripes!" Terry was frowning. Mike and Joe exchanged a look, worried on Joe's side and stern on Mike's.

It was clear that someone had "taken" Andy for three dollars and that he was going to be let down. That was all that the two younger boys saw—and, with Andy's face dreaming in the dim light from below, that was enough. Mike and Joe were beginning to sense something more: some bigger problem, not so simple to grasp.

Joe tried once. "Look, Andy, you know you couldn't really buy Beecham Park for three dollars. It'd cost thousands and thousands."

"The old chap sold it cheap," Andy explained. " 'A packet of trouble,' that's what he said. He wanted to sell it cheap."

Old chap! That was unexpected. Not some mean-hearted member of the high-school set, then; someone older, from whom Andy should have been safe. "Cunning old coot," muttered Terry, and spat.

Andy turned to them, full of delight, the spikes of hair standing up on the back of his head. "Good, isn't it?" he breathed.

"I can't stand this," muttered Mike. "Let's get out of here. We need a bit of time."

"Come on, boy," said Joe, putting a gentle hand on Andy's shoulder. "Time we went home."

Andy followed them up the cliff. "I'll show you tomorrow, too," he promised. "It's real quiet, and you can see the men sweeping her out."

They saw Andy to his own street and watched him loping home. Then, since Joe's front yard was the nearest private place, they wandered that way.

"We never should have let him loose for a whole week,"

said Joe. Andy was a responsibility they accepted.

A woman came to a dimly lit door and shrieked, *"Fred!"*
At an upstairs window two men were shouting angrily. In
the street a white-coated figure strolled among the cars.

"We can't talk to his mother," Mike pointed out. "She
doesn't know he's taken the money from his money box."
Since all their families and most of their friends had known
each other for a long time and met very often, that seemed
to dispose of all adult help. They filed through Joe's front
gate and sat on the steps.

"What do we want to talk to her for, anyway?" said
Matt. "She can't do anything. Andy's been taken for three
dollars, but I don't reckon *she'd* know who did it."

"If they get away with this," Terry pointed out, "they'll
be selling him the Harbor Bridge next."

"We'll have to see about that, won't we? Andy must
know who he gave the money to. We'll have to find out
from him."

Terry smiled fiercely.

"And how are you going to explain to Andy?" demanded Mike. "You saw him back there. Are you just going to tell him he doesn't own the place after all?"

"Poor old Andy," muttered Joe, beating his fist softly on
the step. "He won't believe it."

"He'll get over it in a week or two," Terry suggested.
"If we take him gently till then, there won't be much harm
done."

For once Mike disagreed violently with his younger
brother. "Don't be a lunatic! He'll go around acting as if
he owned the place, making himself a laughing stock. Half

the kids in Appington Hill will be having a go at him."

Matt jumped up impatiently. "He *can't* really believe he owns Beecham Park! How does he think he's going to run it? All those tough types down there—*they'll* tell him pretty quick if we don't. He'll just have to listen to sense for once. I'll tell him myself tomorrow."

"You can try," said Mike.

Matt was a little surprised to find the matter being left to him like this. He stalked home feeling important and very determined. He was waiting for Andy when he called early in the morning and went out with him to the quiet streets.

"Got to pick up the others," said Andy happily. "I bet they want to come." He headed for Joe's back gate, and Matt followed. Andy collected all his friends and took them down to the lower gate of Beecham Park to watch the men sweeping.

"Quiet, isn't it?" he said proudly. "Not like last night."

This was the moment, Matt decided. He caught Terry's glance and frowned importantly.

"Look here, Andy," he began, "where's your sense? You know you couldn't really buy this place for three dollars, don't you?"

"I just did," said Andy, smiling warmly and nodding hard.

"You wasted your money, that's all. How do you think you're going to keep it going? Eh?"

Andy looked at him in a puzzled way and laughed uneasily.

"Come on, snap out of it," urged Matt. "How do you

think you can run the place? What about those men sweeping up the rubbish? They'll be wanting their money in a minute, won't they? What are you going to pay them with? Bottle tops? And what about the men that water the track? And the ticket sellers? You don't think they're going to run around doing your work for you for *nothing?*"

Andy thought deeply. A lot of people had bought tickets last night; and there were the men now, sweeping. "They *are* doing it," he pointed out. "Look, I just showed you. You can see 'em, can't you, Mike? Can you see the men sweeping, Joe?" He nodded earnestly at Matt. "They're doing it, all right. See 'em?"

"But what about the *money?*" shouted Matt.

"Steady on," said Joe. Andy's face was beginning to look stormy. He struggled for words and tried to explain to Matt.

"I *said* about the money already. I told you three dollars, and a long time getting that last one."

Matt took a deep breath and tried coaxing. "Andy, old boy, three dollars is just crazy. Why, what about the new stand, the one they've just put up? That cost *thousands* of dollars, just by itself."

Andy laughed delightedly. "He said I got it cheap! It was a bargain, *I* know." He added kindly, "You don't want to worry about it, Matt. I got no more money, so I can't build no more stands. That one was there already."

Matt gripped a handful of his own dark hair and looked helplessly at the others. They had been listening in a careful, judging way, and now Mike and Joe nodded a little. It was no good badgering Andy like this. Joe felt an urge to take him away from Beecham Park, to keep him away as much as possible and wait a little.

"Where's the skateboard?" said Joe cheerfully. "It's time we had another go. There's that bit of road that goes below the case factory. It's pretty steep, and no one goes there at weekends."

They went to fetch the skateboard. Andy went with them quite happily and watched for the rest of the morning, but in the afternoon he wandered off alone.

5 Inside the Walls

Once Matt had tried to talk sense to Andy and had failed, there seemed to be nothing else that could be done just yet. Matt fumed helplessly. Terry looked dark and scornful, but neither of them could think of anything to suggest. Mike waited grimly for a sign of any new mocking or teasing, for it seemed to him that the cruelest part of this whole cruel trick was that Andy should be made to look a fool—Andy, who couldn't help himself and would never hurt anyone else. Joe's idea, that they should try to keep Andy away from Beecham Park until he forgot his obsession, was the best that anyone could suggest; but it was not as easy to carry out as it seemed. There were so many things to do. It was easy to keep an eye on Andy when he was there, doggedly and loyally following them about. It was not so easy to find him when he was missing, as he often was these days. They always watched for him when they were passing the lower corner of Beecham Park, where the gate often stood open; and once or twice, when they thought of it, they went to the cliff especially to look for him. Yet they saw very little of Andy during the next week.

Andy was not trying to avoid his friends. He would have been very glad to have them with him, but he was too much occupied just now to spend his time following them about. Early in the morning, after school, and in the warm evenings, he wandered about Appington Hill finding places from which to catch a fresh glimpse of his racecourse. So far he was content to look and admire, to see everything that happened, to possess it in his mind. There was still a shyness in the way he approached it—not the shyness of uncertainty, but a shyness brought on by the size and importance of his new world. He drifted quietly from place to place, finding vantage points on both the cliffs, from the height of Wattle Road, through gaps in the fence. Chuckling with pride, he watched the track being watered or raked, seats being repaired in the stands, horses training in the early morning. And he discovered the greyhounds.

In a vague way, he had always known that greyhounds as well as trotters raced at Beecham Park. Like everyone else in Appington Hill, he had often seen them being taken for walks: lean, high-arched creatures walking delicately on long, springing legs and wearing muzzles on their pointed snouts. On the nights they raced, the crowds were much smaller than those at the trotting meetings. The big grandstand remained empty and unlit, and the high whining of the mechanical hare went on and on until it became unnoticeable. Andy was hardly aware of the greyhounds until he watched them racing from his place on the cliff.

He liked the constant baying of the dogs, and the whining and bobbing of the hare. He liked the grass track that sprang up, vividly green under its own circle of floodlights, within the other track. He was amused and touched, chuckling to himself on the cliff, at the fierceness of the dogs straining to catch that little machine that could always put on just enough speed to stay in front, and at the solemn procession of men leading them out to race. Sometimes a fight would break out among the dogs being taken from the course after a race, but it never lasted for more than a moment or two. Andy would laugh hugely, mutter encouragement to the dogs, and admire the way their trainers handled them. On the whole, he found greyhound meetings, or the training nights, more homely and interesting than trotting but not so brilliantly and splendidly exciting.

Even in the streets he began to watch for the gallant creatures that used his racecourse. In the morning he might see one of the horses returning from its training, lively and gentle amid the zooming cars and thundering trucks, drawing its gig with grace and ease up the steep hills that the people climbed so heavily and slowly. In the afternoon he would meet a greyhound with cold, remote eyes, straining against the short leash that kept it in check. Andy watched them proudly and sometimes waved to the drivers or the people leading dogs. Often they waved back, for Andy's open, simple face was warmer and more interested than the faces of most boys. He was delighted when they waved. It seemed as though they knew he belonged.

One night a great black storm came rolling up from the south. Green glares of lightning ripped across Andy's window, flash after flash, tearing darkness and color away. Thunder cracked and crashed, and then the rain thrashed at the roof. All through his sleep he heard crashing thunder, hurtling rain, and the wash and gurgle of gutters overflowing. In the morning the storm-water channel was running full, carrying timber and paper and soggy cardboard out to the harbor. When Andy looked through the gate into Beecham Park, he stood transfixed. The green circle inside the track had become a wide sheet of water, and a company of sea gulls screamed over it or sat on the surface.

That morning Joe was out early, too, chasing the milk-man for an extra pint of milk that his mother had forgotten to order. He came upon Andy staring through the wire mesh of the gate, silent and still. Joe stopped to look, too. The strong white wings of the gulls flashed in the early sun.

"See the birds," whispered Andy, finding a friend beside him. "Birds and dogs and horses. . . . I wish the birds would stay."

"You didn't have to pay three dollars to look at it," Joe reminded him. "You could have looked without."

"I could have looked without," repeated Andy, nodding. He added, "Only now it's mine."

Joe tried again. "Wouldn't you like to have the money back and buy something else? You'd still have this just the same."

Andy's eyes slid away, discarding these words. As far as he could see, they had nothing to do with anything.

"Let us help you get the money back," persisted Joe. "We're friends, aren't we? We'll help, boy."

The warmth of Andy's smile was like the sun coming through a window. "Gee, I know that, Joe. If I need any help, I'll let you know."

Joe turned away helplessly, clutching his bottle of milk. Andy's voice called after him.

"Hey, Joe! I'm real sorry you haven't got a place like

this, Joe. I mean a real place, not kidding like that game.
. . . You can have a share of this any time you like, Joe."

Joe muttered, "Thanks, boy," and went away.

It was when he heard this story from Joe that Terry, that
fierce young O'Day, turned coldly angry. In precise and
considered words he stated that the old man who had sold
Beecham Park Trotting Course to Andy Hoddell was a
mean, miserable, cunning, and rotten old urger. Then he
closed his lips in a thin straight line and went away to look
for Andy.

Joe had told his story on the way home from school. By
then the storm lake had drained away from Beecham Park,
the sea gulls were gone, and the sun had almost dried the
grounds. Terry came upon Andy observing these changes
from the vacant ground above Wattle Road, sitting on his
favorite stone, surrounded by stray cats. Terry stood before him, coldly determined.

"Who's this old geezer that sold you Beecham Park?"

"Him?" said Andy. "I don't know him. He's the bloke
that used to own it."

"You come and find him and show us. He can give you
back that money."

"*I* don't want it back," said Andy, astonished. "I'd rather
have the racecourse. That's why I bought it."

"You listen to me," said Terry sternly. "He never owned
Beecham Park, so he couldn't sell it to you. He's a yellow
dingo taking money off you like that. He's rooked you,
that's all."

Andy began to look lost and lonely. Terry's relentless
voice went on.

"Can't you understand plain English? You had a dirty trick played on you. You've been robbed. You got a right to have that money back again, and you're getting it back. We'll make him give it up."

"You stop it!" shouted Andy, stumbling to his feet. "I don't want that money back when I already spent it, do I?" Stray cats hissed, spat, and vanished over fences. "I had enough trouble buying the place," shouted Andy, "without you messing it up!" He turned and loped quickly away into the lane.

For a day or so Terry kept on searching, determined to make the victim realize his misfortune; but now Andy really was avoiding his friends, darting around corners and into back lanes whenever he saw them coming. He was nervous of Terry.

Both Mike and Joe were annoyed when they heard of this episode. "You went off half cocked," said Mike, accusing Terry. "You ought to have known it wouldn't work. It's useless trying to bounce Andy. He just gets pig-headed."

"You've upset him, too," added Joe. "If you don't watch out, he won't talk to us about it at all. How can we get him out of this mess if we don't know what's going on?"

"I know you were doing your best," said Mike, cutting the argument short now that Joe had entered it. "Anyhow, it can't be helped."

Only Matt sympathized with Terry. "I know just how you feel—you wish you could get behind Andy and *push* him. At least you and I have tried, and that's more than some people I know."

Joe and Mike ignored this reproach. Each of them still

had that feeling of waiting for the real problem to emerge. There was something more at stake than the loss of three dollars, something they didn't yet understand. Meanwhile, they could only go on as they were doing, looking out for Andy whenever they thought of it and not seeing him very often.

Andy continued to avoid them. By now he had gazed at his racecourse from every possible point, and his shyness was beginning to wear off. Sitting on the side of the cliff and looking into the grounds, he began to wonder if the men had swept them properly.

" 'A packet of trouble,' " he would mutter, solemnly shaking his head. "That's what he said. 'A packet of trouble.' "

It had been no trouble at all to Andy. He could have wished it to be a little more trouble, for it hardly seemed to know he was there.

One night when the whine of the mechanical hare went on and on, he ventured down to the open gate instead of going up to the cliff to watch. There was a man standing just inside the gate, a tall man with a strong, long-jawed face and a square mouth. Andy was surprised to see him and halted rather suddenly. Then he gave the man his warm smile, said, "Hello, mister," and leaned against the gatepost. The man looked at him in a serious way that Andy liked and nodded politely.

The hare came whirring by, and the greyhounds bounded after it in long, elastic strides. To stand so near them was something new. Andy chuckled with excitement, looking up at the man in a companionable way, and went on watching. A short-legged ginger pup with a curling tail recognized Andy and came to sit in the gateway. It grinned a happy, silly grin, but Andy was too absorbed to notice.

There were no people in the grandstands and no lights on except the floodlights over the track. There were only the men who were busy with the dogs, and they were not wearing their long white coats. They were on the other side of the course, near the barrier with its little doors that opened to let the dogs out at the beginning of a race. The hare went whining endlessly around the track, going quite slowly some of the time but never stopping. Sometimes, as it passed the barrier, the doors would fly open, and four or five greyhounds would leap after it. Then the hare would put on speed and give them a race. There was a constant yelping and baying.

"It's not proper racing, *I* know," said Andy wisely to the tall man. "Just practicing, that's all it is."

"Training," said the man, nodding.

Then something happened that filled Andy with astonishment and joy. The hare came slowly by, with no greyhounds following. The ginger pup at Andy's feet went running into the ring, yapping in a happy, breathless way— and suddenly, on the emerald-green track under the brilliant lights, the puppy was chasing the hare. Neck stretched out, ears flying, short legs bounding, the puppy was catching up when, just in time, the hare speeded up and escaped. The puppy went after it, yapping eagerly.

Andy roared with laughter. He hit the gate with his hand and roared again. "Look at him go! He nearly got it! He thinks he's a greyhound." He laughed and laughed, looking up at the tall man and pointing at the ridiculous ginger pup.

On the other side of the track, indignant greyhound trainers were waving and shouting. The pup, uncurling its tail a little and beginning to look hunted, swerved away under the rails and disappeared. The tall man's square mouth stretched into a wide smile.

"A nice set-out," he said, giving Andy a sympathetic nod. Then he strolled off toward the stands.

Andy came a little farther inside the gate and sat on the ground. He was glad to have made friends with the tall man. He sat by himself in the dusk, full of the pride of ownership.

On the next afternoon, finding the gate open again, he slipped quietly inside and looked about. There was nobody in sight on all the broad circle of the racecourse. Andy wandered about, noticing details he had never seen before in spite of all his watching—mysterious locked doors under the big grandstand, wooden benches inside the ring where the band sat when it wasn't playing, a long building with a row of little windows like the ticket windows—until he found himself in an open space right under the high walls. It was very quiet and deserted. He felt safe and private inside the walls of the racecourse.

It was not as clean and neat as it seemed from a distance. He collected some old programs, cigarette packets, and wrappings from chocolate bars and put them in an empty rubbish bin. "Ought to keep it tidy," he said, shaking his head. "A packet of trouble, that's what it is."

There was a long garden bed against the wall, with roses and hydrangeas standing tall at the back and a tangle of phlox and dianthus in front. Andy was surprised and pleased to find it there and looked at it for a long time. There were some withered flowers on the plants and weeds growing here and there between them. Andy shook his head again.

"I shoulda come before," he said with some pleasure.

He crouched on the paving in front of the bed and began to pull out weeds and pick off a few dead flowers. After a while he felt that someone was near him. He looked up. It was the tall, sober man with the long jaw and square mouth. He carried a coiled hose over his arm, and he was looking at Andy in the same serious but friendly way as before.

"Just going to give them a drop of water," he said, laying down the hose. He uncoiled one end and took it to a tap farther along the wall. He screwed in the hose, turned on the tap, and came back. Andy sat back on his heels and watched the hose writhe and jump as it took the pressure of water. The man picked up the nozzle and threw a jet of water among the plants.

"You work here, mister?" asked Andy, pulling at another weed.

"Part of the time," said the man. He glanced at the little heap of weeds and dead flowers on the paving and added, "Seems you've been working, too."

"There's a lot wants doing," said Andy, frowning and nodding. "I shoulda started sooner. I picked up a whole heap of papers already. It's a packet of trouble."

"Takes some keeping up, all right," the man agreed.

"I don't know who you are," Andy stated, obviously thinking about it. He liked this quiet, friendly man.

"Name's Bert Hammond. Yours?"

"What—me? I'm Andy Hoddell, that's who I am." He
tried the man's name over. "Bert Hammond—that's Mr.
Hammond, that is." Shyness was making him grab at the
weeds and yank them hard. He wanted to tell the man more

than just his name. He wanted to say what else he was, besides being Andy Hoddell, but the words seemed to be too big. He went back a little way in the conversation so that he could have another try.

"It's a packet of trouble, this place. I shoulda kept an eye on it sooner." He glanced sideways and saw that the man was watching him thoughtfully. He chuckled a few times, and then the words came. "It's *my* place, this. Did you know that, Mr. Hammond? I own it."

The man nodded in a good-humored way. Andy could tell that he hadn't really known at all. He wasn't even listening properly.

"I own the lot," he insisted. "All this. Got it cheap because the old man wanted to get rid of it. Three dollars, and cheap at the price. 'A packet of trouble,' he said it was. It is, too—but I reckon it's pretty good, don't you?"

The man nodded again. He was listening all right now, and Andy chuckled proudly.

"I only had two dollars, and Mum never knew I took that. My own money, it was, out of my box. I never pinched it. Only then I had to get that other one; *that* took me a time. I done everything, getting that money, but I got it. . . . It was worth it, don't you reckon, Mr. Hammond?" He stood up and looked across the wide grounds, and his blue eyes were warm with joy in his racecourse.

"Who sold it to you?" said the man, but he said it in a quiet and friendly voice that was not at all like Terry's. Andy laughed.

"Don't you know? The old man, of course, the one that *used* to own it. He never said his name, but he used to own this place." Suddenly afraid again, he stared with round eyes and with spikes of hair standing up.

"I don't want the money back, Mr. Hammond. Terry says—Joe says—they reckon I can have the money back. What do I want it for? I'd rather have Beecham Park! Wouldn't you rather have Beecham Park? You won't tell Terry and Joe, Mr. Hammond? You won't say who that old bloke is? See, they might ask him for the money back."

"All right, boy. All right. I won't tell them."

Andy laughed with relief. "I better get on with my work."

Bert Hammond took the hose to the farther end of the bed. Andy wandered about collecting more papers. They worked in a companionable way without talking until Andy, who was still remembering how wrong Joe and Terry had been, suddenly remembered something that Matt had said. He raised his head and called.

"Hey! Mr. Hammond!"

"That's me!"

"Do I have to pay you money for doing this?"

Bert Hammond didn't answer for a moment or two. Then he said, "You don't get the money from the gate, do you?"

The money from the gate. That would be the money that people paid to come in and see the races.

"I never got no money."

"There you are, then. Let the ones that take the money pay the bills."

Andy smiled warmly. "That's fair," he said.

6 Andy's Race

After that Andy came quietly into the racecourse whenever he found the gate open. Sometimes he saw Bert Hammond; sometimes there was only a distant figure moving about the grounds or working in the stands; sometimes one or two of the trotters would be working on the track. Andy didn't mind. Bert Hammond had accepted him calmly and quietly, in a way that seemed quite natural. Andy took it for granted that other people who had business at Beecham Park would do the same. They were the people who used the course or kept it in order, and they had a right to be here. Andy owned it, and he had a right to be here, too. He wasn't going to bother them, and they wouldn't bother him.

Sometimes the driver of one of the horses would raise a whip in greeting as he whirled around the track with a beating of hoofs and a shirring of wheels. Andy would wave back very solemnly; and if Bert Hammond were there, he would name the horse and driver.

"Blushing Rose. Good little mare. That's Arthur Waley driving. . . . Here's Bill Foster with Midnight Star. Looks better than he did last month."

Andy would gaze at horse and driver in an absorbed way. He could always recognize them after the first time.

It was this that startled Andy's friends when they saw him again. Since his argument with Terry, they had looked for him several times, but they had never thought of looking inside the racecourse. Then Andy found he had a day free from school because of some important meeting that most of his teachers seemed to be attending. At the busy time of morning when everyone was hurrying to school, it occurred to him to keep an eye open for Matt and Joe and perhaps to walk with them as far as their school. He had forgotten about Terry for the time being, so that when he caught up with all four of the boys at the corner of the street, he gave Terry a hunted look and began to slink away. Luckily, Mike and Joe had already seen him. Since they were uneasy and a little anxious, they gave him a louder and warmer welcome than usual.

"Here's old Andy! Come on, mate. Don't scoot off like that."

"There you are, then, Andy. Haven't seen you about. We thought you must have dropped us."

"Not sick, are you, boy? What's up with school?"

Andy was pleased but embarrassed. He shuffled his feet and smiled at the pavement. Terry, with the sharp words of Mike and Joe still stinging his ears, made a special effort. Looking straight at Andy and searching for a way to undo whatever harm he was supposed to have done, he said very seriously, "Everything all right at Beecham Park?"

Just as seriously, Andy's round blue eyes lifted to Terry's brown ones. He seemed to think for a moment. Then he nodded. A small movement of relief went around the group. Still talking rather more than usual, Andy's four friends started for school while he fell into his usual place a step or so behind.

They turned the corner and began to climb Wattle Road toward the traffic lights. Andy, enclosed in his private world but calm and content again, listened to their voices and watched the rush of morning traffic. Then he saw, stepping quietly and daintily amid the rushing traffic, a horse he knew. He shouted excitedly to his friends.

"Hey, Mike! There's Midnight Star! See him, Joe? Looks better than he did last month. See him, Matt? That's Midnight Star—I know him! That's Bill Foster driving. . . . Hey, Bill! Hello, Bill!"

The four boys, hearing again the familiar call that had been missing for so long, all turned their heads at the first word. Humoring Andy again, they looked obediently where he pointed. Their eyes, falling on Midnight Star who was looking better than he did last month, narrowed a little. Learning that Bill Foster was driving, they looked on uncomfortably while Andy waved and shouted. Poor old Andy was making a show of himself. They cast hidden glances at the driver and prepared to walk on in a careless way. They saw the driver turn his head, catch sight of Andy, nod, and lift his whip in greeting. Matt's eyes widened; Mike's grew still narrower.

"See?" said Andy happily. "I know him. He comes to my racecourse, him and Midnight Star."

The boys walked on in silence until they reached the school, where Andy waved and wandered off. They watched him go.

"My sainted aunt," muttered Matt.

"I bet it was a different horse and driver," said Terry.

"Doesn't matter who it was," Mike pointed out. "Whoever he was, *he* knew *Andy*."

"We'll have to keep more of an eye on him," said Joe in an exasperated way. Mike merely shrugged.

After school Joe announced that he was going to find Andy Hoddell and see what he was up to. Mike shrugged again and said nothing about coming, too. Terry had already promised to give Matt some solid batting practice down in the park, but this was a plan that would take up several afternoons and could just as well begin tomorrow. They looked expectantly at their elders. Mike seemed to have drawn into himself; Joe was frowning. Matt raised his eyebrows in a puzzled way.

Terry curled his lip slightly and said, "Don't forget your bat." It seemed to him that for the time being he and Matt had better stick to cricket in the park and avoid taking sides. The fact that Andy Hoddell was on shouting terms with at least one of the racing drivers from Beecham Park seemed to have affected Mike and Joe in different ways. It was as though Joe wanted to hurry forward, anxious to come closer to Andy, while Mike had taken a step backward to stand farther off.

Joe spent the afternoon alone, looking for Andy. He went to the open gate of Beecham Park and then to the cliffs above it. He looked into all the shops and the vacant ground where Andy often sat with the stray cats. He even went to Andy's front door and, standing on the pavement while Mrs. Hoddell looked up from her work, asked if Andy were about. Mrs. Hoddell's face at once set into anxious lines.

"What—isn't he with you, Joe? Well—if he's not with you, I just don't know *where* he is. Keep an eye out for him like a good boy, will you? I don't like to think of him wandering on his own too much." She pushed the hair back from her forehead with her free hand and sighed.

"I might have missed him," said Joe quickly. "I've been up to the corner shop. I'll look in at home—or O'Days' place. He's probably there."

"I hope you catch up with him, then." She smoothed her face out and smiled. "I just take it for granted he's with you boys. You're all so good with him, and I just don't worry. I can't tell you what it's been to me, having you there—I just don't know how I'd have got on without you. It keeps me busy, you know—the work, and the house, and trying to keep Andy nice so people won't talk. You've been a real blessing, the four of you."

"That's all right, Mrs. Hoddell. We like having him around. Everyone likes Andy."

"He *is* a nice boy, and that's a fact. Old Mrs. Eaton was just telling me the other day what a good boy he's been. A help to me, too, mind you. He *is* a good boy, but now he's getting bigger, it's harder to keep track of him. You can't keep a big boy like that in the house all day. He's lucky to have you four, and I'm glad of the chance to tell you. I appreciate it."

After that, of course neither Joe nor any of the others would have worried Mrs. Hoddell again. They listened uncomfortably while Joe told them about it, looking pointedly at Mike while he did so. They could all see there was no way to explain to Mrs. Hoddell that Andy had bought Beecham Park Trotting Course, that he was on easy terms

with horse trainers, and that he seemed to have little time
for his old friends. They could only hope that no one else
need ever tell her; and even Mike, though he no longer
talked about the problem, continued to keep an eye open
for Andy.

They went for long walks around the walls of the racecourse and looked through the open gate without seeing
him. They hesitated to go inside—they, at least, had not
bought the place. It was only by accident that they happened to be walking past the gate on an evening when the
greyhounds were training and the sound of the hare came
singing from the floodlit track. They glanced in as usual;
there, sitting on the grass a little way inside, was Andy. The
four stood still and then went creeping to the gate. They
were glad to find that there was no one else in sight.

"Andy Hoddell!" hissed Matt, scandalized. "Come on
out of that before you get kicked out!"

Andy looked up slowly, and they were all a little shaken
to see his face. It was alive, absorbed. When Andy's mind
looked out through its closed window, it looked directly.
There were never twenty other ideas jostling the main
one. There was never a curtain of restraint to hide his mind
from other people. When there were other people around,
distracting and confusing him, his mind could rarely con-
centrate in this simple and direct way, so that his friends
were not used to seeing it at all. They stood, surprised and
shaken, waiting for him to notice them.

Slowly, the absorbed look faded, and a warm smile took
its place. Andy jumped up and came to the gate, chuckling
with pleasure to find that his friends had at last dropped
in at Beecham Park.

"Hey! Hear the dogs? Don't they make a noise? You hear them, Joe? They come past real close. They'll be just behind that fence—that's the rails, that is. *Whizz!*" He shook his head and laughed. It was impossible to describe the speed and purpose of the dogs. He said, "Come on; you can come in if you like. *I'm* here, aren't I?"

"You better come out," warned Terry. "They'll be after you."

"I don't bother them," said Andy, "and they don't bother me. . . . There he goes! See him jump! The dogs are coming." Bunched in a mass of striving legs and springing bodies, silently pursuing the hare, the dogs leaped by. Andy exulted. "See 'em go!"

The faces of his friends were interested but reserved. He wanted to show them the fullness of Beecham Park, and he wanted them to know that it was his. He said, "You wait on. Don't go. I'll show you something." He dodged past them through the gate and loped away.

"Here, hold on, Andy—we can't . . ."

Andy turned at the corner and shouted, "Wait there!" Then he disappeared.

The others looked at each other doubtfully. "Are we going to hang about here like a lot of galahs till he gets back?" demanded Matt, vexed.

Mike settled back against the gatepost. "They can't stop us from standing here. We're not going in, are we?"

"He *might* get back," said Terry, "or he mightn't."

Joe frowned at the track and said nothing. They stayed like that, staring at the course, the street, or each other, for several minutes.

"Here he comes," said Matt suddenly. "*My sainted aunt!*"

Around the corner came Andy and a straggling pack of dogs, his friends of the streets and lanes. They were of odd shapes, colors, sizes, and dispositions. A dachshund and a curly-tailed ginger pup frolicked at his heels. Something that looked like an Airedale, but mostly white, trotted along a few feet to the right. On the left, silent and stealthy, sidled two elderly fox terriers. A large black dog with a patch of shiny bare skin on its back loped along behind and grinned cheerfully. In front strutted a very small pup with long creamy hair, a stumpy tail, and a cocky expression. From time to time it looked back to make sure that the rest were still following. All the other dogs ignored it, glancing only at Andy and sidling away from each other. Andy chuckled at them, snapped his fingers occasionally, and waved to his four astonished friends.

"*Now* you'll see. You'll bust laughing."

He stood just outside the gate with his eyes fixed on the track, keeping the dogs by him with an absent-minded whistle and snap of the fingers. Farther down the street, Charlie Willis and another boy were dawdling.

"Andy!" cried Joe, thoroughly alarmed. "What do you think you're doing? You can't bring a pack of strays in here! Do you want to end up in jail?"

The whining of the hare came closer, and the thing itself cruised into sight on the inside of the track. It was traveling at half speed; there were no greyhounds following. Andy spoke urgently to his dogs, and they all milled forward through the gate.

"There he goes, boys—get him! Sick him! On to him, boys!"

The dachshund and the curly-tailed pup at once hurled themselves at the track. The small creamy pup uttered a volley of yelps and scuttered after them. The terriers streaked off, low to the ground and deadly silent. The Airedale and the black dog leaped forward in great, strong

bounds. The whole many-colored pack was strung out on the floodlit green of the track. The whine of the hare went suddenly shrill as it slid forward in a startled way. The creamy pup kept up a shrill yip-yip.

Andy was roaring with laughter. "Look at them go, look at them go! They nearly had him that time!" Terry was chuckling, Mike grinning, while Matt hung onto the gate and laughed nearly as much as Andy. Joe chuckled in a helpless and horrified way with his eyes fixed on the track. The crazy, strung-out field, with the dachshund in front and the silky pup yelping in the rear, swung away into the curve of the track. Meeting a group of angry, shouting men, they swerved under the rails, scattered, and disappeared. The deep, dangerous baying of excited greyhounds drowned the sound of the hare. Andy sat down on the grass inside the gate and went on laughing.

"I'm going," said Mike. "Andy! Come out of that. There's some pretty big blokes over there, and they don't look too pleased. Come on—get a move on!"

"Eh?" said Andy. "What are you going for? Aren't you coming in to watch? Hey, Joe—aren't you coming in?"

"No, I'm not," said Joe sternly. "Come *on*, Andy."

Andy turned away from them with a movement of resignation. He had lost them again. None of their muttered calls seemed to reach him, so they retreated to the corner of the street and watched from there for a minute or two. After that, since nothing seemed to be happening, they went away.

Matt was shaking his head in an astonished way. "Old Andy—would you believe it! What's come over him?"

They walked on for several yards, leaning forward to climb the hill. Then Mike said, "He's bought a racecourse."

Terry curled his lip. "He's wasted his money, then. He'll soon find out what the trainers think of him racing strays."

"I don't know what his mother'd say," said Joe, worrying. "If only there was some way to get to him. . . ." He glanced at Mike, but Mike was staring at the sky, and his face was closed. Joe frowned. Suddenly, he said, "I'll see you blokes later," and turned abruptly into another street. Matt raised his eyebrows at Terry, but no one said anything.

The streets were growing dark as Joe wandered on, full of a slow, helpless anger. He was thinking, "What do *they* care? Who cares about Andy Hoddell? He's only poor old Andy. He's lucky to have us, his mother says. That ought to be good enough for him, having us—he can't expect us to *do* anything for him, can he?"

Then the anger faded into a hurt and diasppointed feeling. "I would've thought you could count on Mike," muttered Joe. He always had counted on Mike; counted on him not only to see the same problems that Joe saw but also to work them out and come up with the right answer. And now, just at the worst moment, Mike closed up and didn't seem to care.

"I'll have to work it out myself, that's all," said Joe, turning into a lane so narrow that there was no footpath at all. Tall fences pressed toward him on each side, and above them rose a shadowy wilderness of back stairs, little balconies behind rotting blinds, lights glowing through colored curtains, the dark masses of roofs and chimneys, and, drawn sharply against the tarnished sky, the sketchy outlines of television antennae. Joe saw none of it. He was trying to work things out.

The problem, it seemed to him, was to make Andy see what was real and what was not. Joe could see that that might be hard for someone like Andy. Easy enough to know that a house was real, or a loaf of bread, for instance; but what about things like atoms or Mount Everest or war? A lot of people never saw those things at all, but they were real, just the same. For someone like Andy, it must often be pretty hard to tell which things were real and which weren't. If someone came along and told him that he owned Beecham Park, how was Andy to know that wasn't as real as atoms? All the more reason, thought Joe, for making Andy understand. Some things were real, and you had to live with them whether you liked them or not; other things weren't, and you couldn't have them even if you wanted to. If you didn't know which were which, you were just going to waste a lot of time and get in a hopeless sort of mess. That was the important thing; the question was, how to explain it to Andy? Joe went on thinking about it until he found himself at his own front gate without knowing how he came there.

Andy himself was still sitting near the track and watching the greyhounds training. In spite of them, his face had its sad, lost look. His friends had come at last and had gone away again. He had tried to bring them into Beecham Park and show them that it was his. He didn't have the words to tell them about it: about misty mornings and horses silently running; rain-soaked mornings and the flashing wings of sea gulls; warm evenings and leaping dogs. He couldn't describe the excitement of floodlit nights or the peace inside the quiet walls on a warm afternoon. He could only try to show them. They had laughed, too, but then they had gone away. He had lost them again. He sat there sadly, watching the dogs, and it was some time before he heard voices calling softly from the gate.

"Andy Hoddell! Hey, Hoddell!"

When he did hear, he looked to see who was calling. In the dusk he could see Charlie Willis and another boy, Ted Chance, grinning and beckoning in the gateway. Andy frowned. They were not friends of his. "I heard you," he said loudly. "What do you want?"

"Who said you could go in there, Hoddell? Come on over here."

"No one said. I just came. I'm staying."

The two boys whispered together for a minute, then crept through the gate and came softly to Andy.

"I never said *you* could come," Andy pointed out. "You got no right."

The boys giggled.

"Aw, come on, Andy. Be a sport—fetch the dogs again!"

"Fetch 'em, boy. We want to see 'em race again."

Andy knew that wheedling, teasing tone. "You seen," he said sourly. "You get out of here."

"I *said* you wouldn't be game," whispered Charlie. "I'll give you two cents."

"You get out of here!" shouted Andy, his face dark. "It's not your place. What do I want your two cents for? Get out."

"Sh!" The two boys giggled uncertainly and peered into the dusk.

"Get off my racecourse!" roared Andy. "I'll have them set the greyhounds on you!"

"Put a sock in it, can't you?" said Charlie anxiously. Ted Chance tugged at his sleeve. They moved silently back to the gate and disappeared.

After a while Andy stood up and went home.

7 Meet the Owner

Andy's disappointment was gone by the next morning. It was a pity that his friends didn't seem to like his racecourse, but they were still the people he admired and trusted. He didn't expect always to understand them. After school he went off contentedly to weed the garden inside the high walls.

He was proud of his garden. There was always a lot of oxalis, and Andy worked hard at getting rid of it because he knew oxalis was a pest; but the onion weed he liked and cultivated as carefully as the flowers. It grew so tall, taller than most of the formal plants, and he liked the way the long hollow stems curved with the weight of their delicate white flowers. He was pleased with his onion weed and was carefully leaning a long stem against a hydrangea for support when he saw Bert Hammond coming with the hose. Andy gave him a wide and welcoming smile.

"Here's a big one," he said, proudly displaying the onion weed. "See the flowers."

Bert Hammond nodded in a companionable way. Andy's gardening seemed reasonable enough to him. If anyone liked weeds as well as phlox, then weeds were as good as phlox and a lot easier to grow. People didn't come to Beecham Park to admire the phlox. As far as Bert could see, an unconventional display in the garden did nobody any harm. Racing was a different matter. That was the serious business of Beecham Park, and an unconventional display on the track mattered very much.

"Reckon I'll have to lock that bottom gate when the dogs are training," said Bert heavily. "Too many strays altogether. There was a whole mob got in last night."

Andy looked a little self-conscious and bent over the garden. "Here's another big one," he said, gently disentangling another long stalk from the choking growth of phlox and raising it among the shrubs. Bert glanced at the onion weed, but his mouth remained uncompromisingly square.

"Trainers don't like a pack of mongrels in the way," he pointed out. "Bad for business. A racecourse is for racing dogs. They'll go to another course. We won't get any dogs."

Andy was alarmed. "They gotta come here! You tell 'em, Mr. Hammond. We don't want no strays here, getting in the way. We'll keep 'em out. You tell the trainers!"

Bert Hammond's mouth relaxed at last. "That's how it is, is it? All right, boy. Don't you want to tell 'em yourself?"

"I don't know 'em that well," mumbled Andy shyly.

"You'll find Wilf Thomas walking Golden Boy in the park any afternoon. I'll tell him to look out for you."

Andy stared at the wall, absorbing this information. A warm, satisfied look spread over his face. Bert went on hosing the bed, and he, too, was satisfied.

On the following afternoon Andy did not go to the racecourse but walked past its walls and down to the open park. He crossed the storm-water channel by a little bridge near the willows and reached the stretch of green that swept down to the arches of the railway, through them, and beyond. Each of the arches made a tunnel of shadow, and in front of one, bright against the darkness, Terry O'Day was giving Matt Pasan some serious batting practice.

They had put up the wicket they had made out of timber from the storm-water channel. Terry was fielding as well as bowling, doing both with silent intensity, his face flushed with heat. Matt, who would not have needed this practice if he could have borrowed some of Terry's intensity, was relaxing at the wicket between balls. It was Matt who saw Andy wandering over the grass, looking about in a vaguely hopeful way.

"There's old Andy!" shouted Matt. "He'll field."

"Maybe," grunted Terry, and bowled a slow one. Matt hit it toward the solid, spiky-haired figure coming slowly from the bridge. It fell with a thud that made Andy jump and rolled quickly on toward the channel.

Andy looked to see who was playing, then trotted after the ball as a matter of course. He threw it, not very accurately, and chuckled with approval as Terry swept down and gathered it up.

Matt shouted, "Thanks, boy. Watch this one!"

Time was important to Andy only moment by moment. Golden Boy was not in sight, but Terry and Matt were. He stayed, contentedly fielding balls and glad to share in the game. The sun dropped behind a ridge, edging with gold the clustering roof-tops and sending long, shapeless shad-

ows across the park. Suddenly, through the dark tunnel
of a railway arch, came a man leading a greyhound.

Andy, who was bringing the ball back from the channel,
saw them at once. He stood and watched as the man and
dog came on past Matt at the wicket; then he loped toward
them. As he was still holding the ball, Matt and Terry
waited uncertainly.

"Hello," said Andy, smiling his warm smile and fixing
his round blue eyes on the greyhound. "That's Golden
Boy, isn't it?"

"That's him," said the man gruffly, walking on. He was
short and broad, with heavy brows. He held the dog's
leash in a strong, aware grip, very much in control. The
sleek tawny dog wore a muzzle on its pointed snout and
looked at Andy with dark, cold eyes.

"You're Wilf Thomas, *I* know," said Andy.

"That's me," said the man. He walked on, and Andy followed a few steps behind, talking to his back.

"Golden Boy goes to Beecham Park. That's my racecourse. We don't want no strays there, mister. They just
get in the way. We gotta have the real dogs."

The man stopped. He looked at Andy with a half-smile
that made his face pleasanter. "Oh. So you're the owner."

Andy chuckled with delight. "That's me."

"Bert Hammond told me to look out for you. Here—
want to lead him for a bit?"

Andy hesitated, chuckling and turning pink. "He can't
do no harm, can he? He's got that thing on his head. Will
he go steady?"

"He'll be all right. I'll have an eye on him." Wilf

Thomas was holding out the leash. Andy discovered that he
still had the cricket ball.

"I forgot," he said in great surprise, and turned to look
for his friends. They were a few feet away, watching intently. Matt's mouth had dropped open a little, and Terry

was frowning at the greyhound. "Here's your ball," said Andy. "Thanks for the game. I gotta go."

He took the leash, twisting it twice around his hand as Wilf Thomas showed him. Wilf spoke to the dog, and they went away over the grass toward the bridge. The dog walked ahead, its long legs moving lightly. Andy's whole mind was fixed on the dog as he followed it. The man walked beside him with a hand ready to take the leash if necessary. They went over the bridge and out of the park. Peeping from the storm-water channel, Charlie and Greg Willis watched them go.

When they had disappeared, Terry O'Day began pulling up the stumps of the wicket. Matt was staring in a dazed way.

"The owner! Did you hear that?"

"Of course I heard. They've started pulling his leg."

"Didn't sound like that to me," said Matt.

He said so again the next morning on the way to school. "I don't reckon that chap was pulling Andy's leg—he looked a grouchy sort to me. He wasn't even going to talk till he found out who it was. Then he said, 'Oh, you're the owner,' and handed over the dog, just like that."

The others listened, Mike distant and unmoved, Joe with a heavy frown. Neither of them said anything. Matt shot a puzzled look at each in turn.

"I don't know what's up with you blokes lately," he ventured. "Anyone'd think we'd had a blazing row about poor old Andy. I thought we all felt the same way."

"What way?" demanded Terry with a twist of his mouth.

"Well . . . there's poor old Andy, lost his money, thinks he's done something wonderful, and he's going to come an awful cropper. We can't get his money back because he won't tell us who pinched it; and we can't make him give up all this rot because he won't take any notice of us, and he's getting in deeper all the time. But we *would* do something if we could, wouldn't we? We'll have another try first chance we get, so we want to know what's going on. That's right, isn't it?"

Joe said nothing but looked at Mike. Mike shrugged. Joe flushed angrily.

"Yes," said Joe. "It *is* right—only it's not the money that matters so much."

This seemed to reach Mike. He looked up and said, almost unwillingly, "What is it, then?"

"The other part. He really *believes* he owns Beecham Park, and he's getting in deeper all the time. He's got to come out of it. He'll just have to wake up to himself."

"Why will he have to?" said Mike.

"Because it's not real, of course. How can he go on getting wrapped up in something that's not real?"

"Real?" said Mike. "What's real? The trainers speak to him in the street and let him lead their dogs and call him the owner. That's real, isn't it? He goes into the course whenever he wants to, and nobody stops him. That's real. He took a bunch of strays to greyhound training and put on a race of his own. Wasn't that real?"

"Come off it!" snorted Joe. "I don't know what's biting you, O'Day. It seems as if you don't care what happens. Andy—Mrs. Hoddell—after all this time— You don't think it's *right*, do you? What's going to happen in the end?"

Mike blazed back. "I don't *know*, see? I'm not like some
people that always know what's right and what's going
to happen! I just don't know."

Matt stared in astonishment from one to the other. The
blazing row seemed to be happening after all. Even Terry,
carefully saying nothing, still had that bitter twist to his
mouth. "I wish someone would tell me the score . . ."
Matt was beginning, when he was interrupted by voices
from behind.

"O'Day! Hey, Mooney! Wait a sec!"

All four swung around to look. The Willis boys and
Ted Chance were hurrying up the hill, calling as they came.

"Hang on a bit, you jokers! We want to ask you something."

Andy's four friends stood and waited. The newcomers
came up, breathing heavily. Greg started talking even before he reached them.

"Wanted to ask you something. What was that down at
Beecham Park, all those strays the other night? Charlie
reckons you were there. That Andy Hoddell, the soft one,
was acting as if he owned the place, and nobody booted
him out or anything." He grinned expectantly.

Andy's friends shifted a little, standing together. The
blazing row seemed to be over. Terry said, "If Charlie was
there, he'd have seen as much as we did. Didn't he?"

"Yeah—but what's the strength of it? You ought to
know—Hoddell's always hanging round after you lot. Did
he just barge in? What's he doing exercising greyhounds in
the park?"

"He's got a lot of friends," said Mike. "A lot of people like Andy. He's a decent sort. Doesn't poke his nose into other people's business."

"He's got too much sense," added Terry.

"Trainers and blokes like that trust him," explained Matt.

"He's a good sort all right," said Joe. "He'd be sure to have a lot of friends."

"Bound to," agreed Mike. They nodded earnestly at each other. "I'd be sorry for anyone who upset Andy Hoddell."

The Willis boys and Ted Chance shifted their feet. "Who's upsetting him?" They strolled past toward the school. "Just thought you might know something . . ."

"Windbags," muttered Terry. Andy's friends strode on in a body. The Willis boys would never have guessed that anything divided them.

Neither was Andy troubled by such an upsetting idea. It was sad that his friends didn't like his racecourse, but he scarcely had time even to remember that. The weekend was coming around, and he had heard from Bert Hammond that the trotters were racing on Friday night as well as Saturday. It had come into Andy's head to go down on Saturday morning and help the men clean up. The thought of it made him a little shy, for he didn't want to be a nuisance to the men; but he thought that, with two lots of sweeping to be done, they wouldn't mind if the owner helped.

"They could do with some help, I reckon," muttered Andy hopefully.

He woke early on Saturday morning and, borrowing an

old broom of his mother's from the back yard, went down to the lower gate of Beecham Park. The streets were still very quiet, but near the course they were littered with papers and rubbish. Andy chuckled at this sign of the crowds who had milled about last night.

The gate was still padlocked, but there was no barbed wire on top. He slid his broom over the gate and let it fall inside, then climbed over himself. The wide course was empty. There was a good deal of litter in front of the big stand, but this was not where Andy had seen the men sweeping. He picked up his broom and walked around, past the garden where his onion weed bloomed, to the farther side of the grounds. He passed long rows of closed windows where people collected tote winnings on race nights, and two shuttered stalls, and the cluster of small red stands that the bookmakers used, until he reached the one low grandstand on this side of the course. The ground on this side rose toward the hill behind, and the grandstand was only a long roof covering rows of wooden benches that rose one behind the other on the sloping ground. Below the rails that edged the track, the rising ground had been cut away so that the track itself remained level. Andy paused beside the rails to look down at the track below. Then he turned and looked the other way.

No wonder it took so many men to sweep this side of the grounds. Somebody must clean up the other side, too, but the litter was far worse here. Andy looked at it in awe. The asphalt was covered with crumpled newspapers, torn programs, cigarette packets, orange peel, apple cores, bus tickets, and every kind of rubbish that people can drop. Be-

ginning just where he happened to be standing, Andy began
to sweep.

Soon he had swept together a small heap of rubbish that
his worn, soft broom could hardly move. He left it
there and swept more rubbish toward it. He had built quite
a mound of litter when he heard a noise of padlocks and
bolts. He paused, waiting, until a man in overalls came in
sight from behind one of the stalls. When he saw Andy, he
stood still for a moment, then came slowly toward him.

"How did you get in here?" asked the man sternly.

"Climbed in," said Andy, flapping his broom at the
ground. "You could do with a hand, I reckon."

The man looked at the heap of rubbish and back at Andy.
"That's all well and good, but where do you get the idea
you can come climbing in here when you like?"

Andy chuckled. " 'Course I can. It's mine. I bought it."
His blue eyes looked kindly and directly at the man, not
blaming him for his mistake. "I won't bother you, mister.
I just came to help."

"Oh . . ." said the man. He looked at Andy in a troubled way, then turned and went back to the stall. Andy
went on sweeping.

Three more men came out from behind the stall. Two of
them had large brooms, very different from Andy's, and
the third had a shovel and a large bin. Andy watched them
begin to work. The brooms were broad, with short, hard
bristles, rather like large scrubbing brushes on handles.
The men pushed them along in a strong, competent way,
clearing the ground section by section, building up mounds
that the man with the shovel lifted into his bin. Andy went

back to his own haphazard method, sweeping very hard and raising a cloud of dust.

More men arrived with brooms or shovels. There were fleeting glances at Andy, thoughtful, inquisitive, or amused. Whenever he happened to catch one of these glances, he nodded and smiled. The glance turned into a friendly nod, a teasing grin, or a sober stare. Most of the time Andy just kept on working, careful to keep out of the way. His heap of litter had grown so big that he looked at it helplessly, not sure what to do about it.

The man who had arrived first, the only one who had spoken to him so far, saw this and shouted, "George!" A man with a shovel looked up, then came over to Andy. He was small, brown, and wrinkled, with bright, quick eyes. He grinned and began to shovel up the rubbish. Andy watched.

"It's the people who come to the races makes this mess, *I* know," he said.

"Makes you wonder, don't it?" said the man.

"There was a lot of 'em last night."

"Were you here? Saw Magic Moment get beaten, did you?"

"No," said Andy. He felt a need to explain this, so he added, "I might come tonight. I can come whenever I like. I don't have to pay."

"So I hear," said the man. "They make *me* fork out every time, but I reckon you're different." Seeing that one or two of the giant brooms were working nearer, he shouted, "Watch it, you blokes! You'll have the owner tipped in with the garbage if you don't mind out."

The men grinned. Andy chuckled and took his old broom to a safer place at one side of the sweepers. He worked on contentedly, and now the men spoke to him when they came near.

"Bit of an honor, having the owner down."

"Thanks for the help, boss."

"See you at the gate tonight. They tell me you're coming down to look the place over."

"Watch it, Fred. This is the owner we've got here."

"Yeah, Bert Hammond was saying."

They spoke kindly, welcoming him. Andy smiled and swept all the harder, always careful to keep out of the way, but inwardly he was swelling with delight and happiness. After a while he noticed that the sweepers were standing and resting on their brooms. The bins were being carted away. The work was finished.

Andy followed the men who were drifting away behind the stall. There was a little room where they were stacking their brooms and shovels. Andy stacked his broom with the others and went out through an open door in the wall. The man who had arrived first stood by, waiting to lock the door when everyone had gone.

"See you later, mate."

"I'll look out for you tonight."

Andy waved and ran off. He reached the vacant ground where the cats lived and paused to chuckle. "The owner. That's who I am. *They* know."

8 *The Splendid Reality*

In the evening of that day, Andy set out for his favorite spot on the cliff. He was dreaming that perhaps he really would go to the races, as he had told the cleaners in the morning. Perhaps, tonight, he would come down from his dark perch on the cliff and plunge into all the brilliance and noise below. The thought of it made him breathe hard, as though he had been running. It was one thing to own the racecourse in a quiet way, watching it and talking to the men who worked there. It was quite another thing to go striding into the middle of it under all the lights, where crowds of people could stare at him. Andy was going to sit on the cliff and dream about it.

Cars were flowing in rivers down Blunt Street and Wattle Road, spreading over the flat ground near the course and banking up into all the streets and lanes above. All the white-coated men were at their busiest. "No, no!" they shouted to flustered drivers. "You won't do it! Forward again . . . now, back . . . back . . . now, around—keep going!" Horse floats went slowly down the hills. Buses, waddling among the lighter traffic like elephants, went down to join the herd in their own parking area. The sky was a mysterious glowing gray made up of violet, lilac, and faded rose. Over the rim of Blunt Street, a neon sign that stood above the city made sharp green flashes against the glowing gray.

Andy went quietly through his little alley and down to the rocks of the cliff. He sat there, looking at the lighted stage below and the crowds that were already drifting there; and he dreamed of himself drifting among them. He didn't hear anyone coming until someone arrived beside him on the rocks.

"Shove over," said Joe, pushing onto the ledge.

Andy's voice was full of pleasure. "Hey, it's you, Joe! Plenty of room here, Joe. Did you come to watch?" The toy figures of the bandsmen marched on the track, and the music came up to them. "Good, isn't it?" said Andy with simple pride.

"Not bad," said Joe cautiously. He had waited for Andy and followed him here, away from stray dogs and silently scornful Irishmen, slipping off while the O'Day boys were finding customers for their back-yard parking space. He had a difficult job to do, and he was going to watch every word with the greatest care. He sat beside Andy, quietly watching while the sometimes silent, shabby racecourse put on its hidden truth of color and life.

"I bet they're making a mess," said Andy happily. "She was cleaned up good this morning, *I* know. I helped." He looked sideways at Joe in the gathering dusk, to see if he were impressed. Joe shifted uneasily on the rock. "They got two lots to clean up this time," Andy went on, "so I gave 'em a hand."

The voice from the amplifier spoke, heralding the first

race. The crowd began to wash along the rails or drain away into the stands. The band disappeared. Andy gave a cry of delight.

"The horses! See the horses!"

The horses and silk-clad drivers went by, and Andy's heart went with them, snatched away under the golden lights, whirling around the track. Joe watched with him, while the great voice sang and the signals flashed, until the race broke and fell apart into flying units and Andy's heart returned to his body.

"Dogs are all right," said Andy, breathing deeply. "Only horses are better."

"Do you like the horses best?" asked Joe. "Best of the whole show, I mean?"

Andy thought about it. "I might do," he said at last.

"But they're not yours, are they? You don't own the horses?"

Andy shook his head solemnly. "They're none of 'em mine. I know most of 'em, though."

"But you don't own them. They're not part of *your* show. What do you like next best? The dogs?"

"Dunno," said Andy, sounding a little confused. "I reckon the dogs are pretty good."

"Do you own them?"

" 'Course not," said Andy, beginning to grow impatient. "You know I got no dogs."

"So you like the horses and dogs best, but you don't own them. What else do you like, then? What's the next best?"

"See the numbers going up," said Andy, sliding away from these pointless and bothering questions. "It's a big night, *I* know. All those people, that's why it's a big night. Hey, Joe, did you ever see such a big night? I reckon there's thousands, don't you? Thousands of people."

"Is that what you like next best?" said Joe relentlessly. "The people? I suppose you don't reckon you own *them?*"

Andy laughed. "You must be crazy, Joe! Nobody owns people." He laughed again.

"All right," said Joe tensely. "So we've got that far, then. You don't own the horses or the dogs or the people. You don't own the cars and buses, either, do you? You don't own the money or the men that do the sweeping." He stopped to take a breath and to force himself to calm down. "I don't see how you own much at all, do you? Nothing very good, anyway. All the best parts, you don't own them at all. I mean, you said so yourself."

"I never said I did!" cried Andy stormily. "I never said any of that—the horses—the dogs . . ." He struggled with the words that came crowding into his mouth. "I told you—all I said—I said, *I bought Beecham Park!*"

"Steady on, boy," said Joe. "I'm trying to work it out for you, see? I mean, if you don't own any of the best bits, it doesn't matter much, does it? What's the good of Beecham Park without the horses and dogs and people? What do you want with it, without that?"

"But they're *there!*" cried Andy. He thrust fiercely with his hand at the scene below. "Can't you see 'em? *There* they are."

"Put a sock in it, Andy—listen, can't you? Of course I can see them. I can see them just as good as you, and I never reckoned *I* owned Beecham Park. So what's the difference if *you* don't own it either? You can see it, just the same as me. What's the difference if you own it or not?"

"I don't know if it's any difference," said Andy. He sounded hopeless and sullen. "I just own it, that's all."

"Don't kid yourself, boy. *I* don't own it, and I'm looking at it, too. You don't own it either, not really. That old chap was just kidding, to get your money out of you."

"You don't know nothing—you wasn't even there! It wasn't kidding—not like that game you play with the gas works and the Manly ferry and all of that. You never owned that stuff, *I* know. You never bought it at all, not like me. You don't want me owning Beecham Park, that's all it is."

· "Andy—Andy, boy. If it was mine, I'd give it to you. But it's not real, boy. You'll find out you've got no Beecham Park and no money either, just nothing. You've got to know what's real, or they'll take it all from you. Look, will you ask your mum? Will you listen to her? She'll tell you the same."

"What does she know? She wasn't there, no more than you." Andy tried for more words, choked, and tried again. "I got gardens down there, with flowers and that onion weed. They're mine. I grew that onion weed . . ."

"Three dollars is a lot to pay for a bit of onion weed. Is that all you've got?"

Andy struggled to his feet. "Come on," he said fiercely. "I'll show you." He started off, scrambling and tumbling down the cliff with an agonized, clumsy speed. Joe hesitated for only a second, then went climbing and sliding after him. He mustn't lose Andy now that they had come so painfully far in this fierce, wrestling argument. He hoped that it might be finished, once and for all, tonight.

They reached the pavement of Wattle Road behind a line of parked cars. Across the road there were lights, parked buses, and groups of people. Andy loped along on the darker side, with Joe following, until he reached the corner of Blunt Street. They both paused there, waiting for a chance to cross, and that was when Mike O'Day saw them from the other side of Blunt Street.

Mike was wandering aimlessly, alone and out of sorts. Terry and Matt had gone off to the workshop together as soon as the yard was full of cars and without inviting Mike to join them. Mike knew they were baffled by the disagreement between himself and Joe. He didn't blame them, for he was baffled, too—but it hurt, all the same. He missed Terry, and he missed Joe. When he saw Andy and Joe across the street, he almost turned back. Then he saw their faces. He frowned and walked across the street toward them.

"Hi, there," said Mike. "Going somewhere, Andy boy?"

Andy scowled at him. "You coming, too? Come on, then. *I'll* show you."

"Good show," said Mike, shooting a hard look at Joe and receiving one in return. They both followed Andy across Wattle Road to the turnstiles of Beecham Park, where he hovered for a moment.

Groups of people were clustering about the turnstiles or drifting through them, giving up their tickets as they went. Andy wandered along the row, looking at the faces of the men on the turnstiles and drawing back when anyone else

came near. At last he made a dart at one of the turnstiles
and spoke to the man in charge.

"You know me, mister?"

The man gave him a friendly nod. "Hello, it's the owner.
Coming in to have a look, boss?"

Andy nodded. Then he jerked his head at Mike and Joe
who stood close behind, uncomfortable but determined.
"These others are coming in, too. They're my friends."

The man hesitated. "Friends, are they? Well, I don't
know. It's different with you—and we don't sell tickets to
kids, of course—but I don't know if I can let half the kids of
Appington Hill come through without they come with
their parents. Can I, now? That's not reasonable, boss."

Andy considered. "I never said that," he pointed out.
"These two, that's all I said. I gotta show 'em. Half the kids
of Appington Hill, I reckon that's not reasonable. I only
said these two."

"Well . . ." said the man. He took his hand from the
turnstile. "I'm not having any trouble with your dads,
that's all. I never saw you."

They pushed between the wire barriers. Joe muttered
"Thanks, mister," as he passed.

"Don't try it on next week," the man warned him. "Tonight you're with the owner—that's the difference."

Again Mike looked hard at Joe, and Joe frowned back.

They came through a narrow passage from the turnstile,
and they all stood still. Even Andy had never seen Beecham
Park like this before. At first they hardly saw the drifting
crowds, the boys selling programs, the rows of little windows where people were placing bets. In front the ground
sloped down to the blazing oval of the track with a pool

of darkness inside it. From here the darkness looked much blacker than it did from above; there was only a glimmer here and there from the cars parked inside it. Beyond this circle of darkness and brilliantly lit track rose the big grandstand on the other side of the course. Its shape outlined with strings of lights, it seemed to float in a magical way above the course, the long rows of seats mounting tier above tier. The boys stared at it for a long moment, floating there against the rose-gray sky. When Andy turned to his friends, the driven look had gone from his face. It glowed again with the enchantment of the racecourse.

"I said I'd show you," he said simply. "There's more than onion weed."

He wanted to show them the onion weed, too, and the bookmakers' stands, and the room where his broom was locked away with the others; but wherever they turned, there was the excitement of race night snatching Andy away. Joe and Mike followed him from place to place, half dazed with listening and looking.

"There's my gardens. Can't get around—they've locked the gate. I never knew about that gate. See, Joe? That cuts her in half, that does. See where they get their money, Mike? See, Joe? The bookmakers—"

They listened to the bookmakers and watched the crowd placing bets. There were men in sports jackets, women in floating frocks and sparkling brooches; there were men in crumpled shirts and shorts, and women who might have stepped straight out of their kitchens. There were babies in prams and small children wandering among the crowds. A man with a bruised face was led off by a policeman.

"The band—see them, Mike?"

They watched the band marching and playing on the other side of the track. There were two very small bandsmen, two who looked very old and feeble, several with red stripes on their dark blue trousers, and several others with gold braid on their sleeves. They were a mixed lot. No one seemed to listen to them. There were young couples who stared at everything, people who walked primly in order to be stared at, men and women staring vacantly at nothing, and bored children who wanted to go home.

"I'll show you where I did the sweeping. . . ."

They walked along the white rails toward the shabby old stand on this side of the track. There were glasses of beer standing on posts and white light beating down on the gritty surface of the track. They reached the place where the ground rose above the leveled track and stood against the rails looking down.

"They'll come real close," said Andy solemnly. "We'll see them all right."

A car came slowly around the track and stopped below the spot where the boys hung over the rails. A man got out. He was an expensive-looking man in a sleek suit and a wonderful bowler hat. He disappeared below the rails, and the car drove on without him.

"A car always comes," said Andy, puzzled. He leaned out as far as he dared, craning to see. Then he burst into loud, surprised laughter and drew back. "You know what, Joe? Hey, Mike, you know what? He's got a little seat that he sits in, all by himself! I never knew that!"

"Shush!" said Joe, but Mike was leaning out to look. Sure enough, there was a small seat built into the bank. The expensive-looking gentleman sat primly perched below the rails and above the track.

"He's there to see that nobody cheats," Mike guessed. Andy laughed heartily.

Horses and gigs began to appear on the track, and the voice came from the amplifiers. A crowd came pressing around the boys, pinning them to the rails, waiting silently. Mike, Joe, and Andy looked along the track, waiting for the horses to come.

"*Mysterious Stranger*," chanted the amplifiers. "*Black Velvet—My Conscience—Lucky Jim . . .*"

"I know him!" cried Andy. "I know a lot of 'em."

The crowd stirred. With a rustling and drumming, the horses sprang into view spread wide across the track. Powerful, beating forelegs, deep, straining chests, and rolling eyes, they hurtled along the track straight at the boys. The three of them hung silent and breathless on the rails with the crowd packed around them. The voice from the amplifiers chanted on. A man waved a glass and called, "*Come* on, fellers, *come* on," as if he were tired of arguing with the drivers. Cockaded heads high, the fierce horses passed. The drivers in their shining satin were perched above whirling wheels. The horses swung toward the inner rail and flowed in a dark stream around the curve.

"*Come* on, fellers," pleaded the man with the glass.

The stream of horses flowed by on the farther side of the track. Here and there, voices shouted to them as they passed. Then they were coming again in a great, strong rush, driving forward so that the boys could scarcely breathe.

"Aw *come* on, fellers."

Around the track again, and a string of red lights flashed as they passed the big stand. The amplified voice grew frenzied and was almost drowned by the roaring of the crowd. They went by like dark thunder, whips flashing and drivers' faces grim; and around the track the roar of the crowd traveled with them. This time a white light flashed, and the horses went flying separately, slowing and turning one by one. The race was over.

The crowd began to break and separate. For a moment the three boys stood where they were in silence. Then Andy turned with a dreaming face and was surprised to see Joe and Mike. He laughed and said, "I forgot."

"Don't blame you," said Mike. "That was really something."

Andy chuckled happily. "Don't you reckon it was really something, Joe?"

"Sure, I do—but you don't own the horses, do you, boy?"

"He's not talking about the horses," said Mike shortly. "He's talking about the race."

"That's right," said Andy. "That's what I said. The race."

Joe and Mike looked darkly at each other. Andy was watching the track.

"Here's that car. I bet the man's going back in it." He craned over the rail. "He's got off his little chair. . . . There he goes."

Mike said, "Come on—we'll have some chips from that stall. My shout, Andy. You brought us in."

Andy chuckled shyly, and they went to the stall. They had to wait while two or three other people were served.

"That's where I did the sweeping," said Andy. "Hey, Mike, did you know I helped sweep her out this morning? There's a place behind here for the brooms, only they're locked up now. Mine and all." Mike hadn't heard about the sweeping, so he explained again. "They liked having the owner down, *I* know."

"Oh," said the woman in the stall, "so *you're* the owner, are you?" The other customers had gone, and she was smiling broadly at Andy. "I heard you were down tonight. After your rent, eh?" She reached across to a shelf and gave Andy a large bag of potato chips. "That do?"

"I got no money," said Andy, hesitating and looking at Mike.

"That's all right," said the woman. She was young and plump, with a mass of yellow hair swathed and looped around her head. "You don't have to pay. That's the owner's rent for the stall."

Andy laughed with surprise and pleasure. "I never knew," he told her, and stood chuckling while Mike bought two more bags for himself and Joe.

"Look, boy," said Mike when the young woman was serving another customer, "it's been great, and thanks for bringing us, but I reckon we better go now. We have to get home. Coming?"

"All right," said Andy. "We can come any time. I don't have to pay, see. I'm the owner." He followed Mike and Joe out through the big roller door that was opened between races.

Mike and Joe walked with him in silence to his own street. Andy went dreamily, full of warm content. He had gone boldly into his racecourse when it was alive, and it had been quite wonderful. His friends had gone with him and seen it all. Now they knew.

"See you," he said, nodding good night, and went loping away in the dark behind a wall of parked cars.

Mike turned on Joe. "Well?" he said sternly.

"Well, what?" said Joe, almost choking with anger and despair. When Mike didn't answer, he burst out angrily. "I nearly had him till you came along, pulling his leg like the rest of them. I hope you're satisfied, that's all. I nearly had him talking sense."

"*Your* sort of sense," said Mike in the same cold, precise tone that Terry used when he was angry. "It seems to hurt pretty bad. I didn't like that, Mooney. I didn't think you'd do that to Andy."

"Do what? Try and get him out of a mess, do you mean? That's one thing *you're* not doing, anyhow, O'Day. *You* don't have to blame yourself."

"I haven't seen anything I *can* do—or you either. What's the *good* of upsetting him like that? What's the use of you telling him one thing when the whole of that mob down there keep showing him you're wrong?"

"I'm *not* wrong. So they can't be showing him, can they?"

"Haven't you got a brain in your head, Joe Mooney? You're so sure that you know everything and poor old Andy's just a lunatic. Can't you shift out of your own light and have another look? Can't you see that *Andy Hoddell owns Beecham Park?*"

Mike turned on his heel and strode off, leaving Joe staring after him in the dark.

9 *The Fame of Andy*

Now it seemed to Joe that the whole world had gone crazy and he was the only sane person left. He and Mike O'Day were the two people Andy trusted most, the two who had looked after him for years. Now, when Joe was doing his best to pull Andy out of this mess, what happened? Andy looked at him as if he were a murderer or something—and Mike O'Day backed him up. Everyone was backing Andy up. The trotting drivers, the dog trainers, the cleaners, the men on the turnstiles, the woman in the stall, and even Mike himself—all of them had slipped away out of reality, into Andy Hoddell's dream. Moodily, Joe kept out of their way, staying at home or wandering by himself. They were all mad, and only Joe himself had any sense.

"Or else *I'm* mad," muttered Joe, kicking at the fence. There were one or two times when he wasn't sure which it was, but it didn't seem to make any difference.

And now that Joe had given up the whole problem in a sullen, defeated way, now that he no longer went hunting for Andy to keep an eye on him, Andy often came looking for Joe. Andy could tell that his friends had quarreled and that the quarrel had something to do with him. He knew how people felt when they were moody and miserable, though he wasn't very clear about the quarrel itself. Joe had been telling him something upsetting and rather frightening when Mike had come along; and Mike could see that it was all right about Beecham Park. Andy was glad of Mike, but still. . . . "Poor Joe. Poor old Joe." Andy wanted Joe to know that they were still friends, that it didn't matter about owning Beecham Park, that it was all right.

"Where you going, Joe?" he would call, spotting the lonely figure with slumped shoulders and pursuing it heavily into some lane. "Can I come? Wait on, Joe." Or he would just appear and follow silently, the usual step or two behind. Since Joe had always been the most patient of Andy's friends, he could not shake off this friendly pursuit. The very core of his hurt was that Mike had accused him of cruelty. He could never be deliberately cruel to Andy. So it happened that for several days Joe spent a good deal of time alone with Andy and was forced to notice small, peculiar things.

There were the men who were always sitting in a row on the long step outside the bar of the hotel. They always shifted and looked more alive when Andy came by. "Hel-*lo*, it's the owner himself. How y' going, mate? . . . Good on you, mate, you show 'em! . . . I've bought the place meself a dozen times, but they never give it to me!"

Andy would nod and chuckle as he passed, then steal a glance at Joe to see if he minded.

There was the time in Ma Eaton's shop when a strange

man came in and greeted Andy warmly. "Afternoon, boss."

Ma Eaton gave Andy a long, sad look, full of pity. "Poor, poor boy," she whispered to the stranger. "Tragic."

Andy rolled his head from side to side in an idiot fashion,

stomped out of the shop, and waited on the pavement. The man looked straight at Ma Eaton from under heavy brows.

"Don't you worry about him, sweetheart," he said strongly. "He's got a lot of friends, that kid has. Good blokes, most of them, even if they are a bit rough. They'll see he's all right."

Ma Eaton sniffed and closed her mouth into a thin line.

On another day they met a woman leading a greyhound, and Andy spoke to her with confidence. "That's Pretty Sal, *I* know. Can I take her a little way?"

The woman, who was short and dark and wearing slacks, handed him the leash at once and walked on beside him. After a minute she said kindly, "You don't want to get messing about with horses and dogs for a while yet. You want to grow up a bit first. Why don't you give it up, eh? Later on you can get a job in the stables or kennels and learn properly. Then you can get yourself something."

Andy laughed in astonishment. "Gee, I don't have to waste all that time; I got it now! I don't reckon you know much about Beecham Park."

"Don't you, now?" said the woman, laughing herself and shaking her head. She let Andy hold the greyhound's leash until they reached the corner of the street.

"Who was *she?*" asked Joe when she had gone. He thought she was a sensible woman.

"I don't know her," said Andy. "Pretty Sal, that's the one I know."

After all, thought Joe, the woman had had no better luck with Andy than Joe himself. She was just another stranger who knew about Andy Hoddell.

A surprising number of people seemed to recognize him in the street. Some of them would just stare at him curiously, but a lot of them smiled or spoke. After a while Joe began to notice a special twinkle in the smiles and a special good humor in the voices. The people who lived in these crowded terraces, the women who hung out their washing in back yards like damp little wells, and the men in shabby jackets who caught early buses in the morning and crowded into the hotel in the evening were glad that Andy Hoddell had bought Beecham Park Trotting Course for three dollars. It was as if a happy chuckle ran through all the twisting streets.

Andy didn't notice this particularly. He was simply pleased to find the world so friendly and would chuckle happily in reply. Then he would make excuses to Joe, in case he minded.

"See, they know I'm the owner. That's all it is."

But Joe's sullen anger was pierced again by anxiety. Andy was certainly famous. At this rate, Mrs. Hoddell couldn't help hearing the story soon.

Would that be a bad thing or a good one? Should Joe go on worrying about it, hoping that it wouldn't happen? Or should he go himself and tell her the story at once? He found himself wishing he could talk it over with Mike— and thinking that perhaps Mike had been right all the time. Perhaps, in a queer sort of way, Andy really did own Beecham Park. Mike had certainly been right about one thing: Joe no longer knew what he ought to do.

On Saturday night Joe walked down Blunt Street and stared moodily at the crowd of race-goers. The big stand, shadowy within its outline of lights, rose against the sky,

and Joe knew that Andy would not come looking for him
tonight. He would be somewhere around Beecham Park,
probably on the cliff above it. Joe stared for a while and
then turned away, deciding that he might as well go home.
He took a few steps up the hill—and found himself face to
face with Mike, Terry, and Matt. They stared at each other
for a minute in silence; then Joe moved forward to pass,
and the other three stood aside. Joe took five or six steps
and suddenly turned back. The others were still standing
against the scaly brick wall, watching him. Joe strode down
and stood face to face with Mike.

"All right, all right," he said, choking angrily. "You
were right. I don't know what to do. Everybody knows
him, everybody. They all talk to him—they all call him
the owner. Maybe he is, *I* don't know—but his mother's
got to hear about it soon, if you're interested. *I* don't know
what to say to his mother, and I s'pose *you* don't care."

Mike said, "Steady on, boy," in the same tone that Joe
often used to Andy. Terry was frowning, and Matt shuffled
his feet, full of concern. It was so good to see them there,
all three of them, just the same as ever, that Joe's anger went
off in a rush and he had nothing left to say.

"Don't strip your gears," said Mike kindly. "We all care;
you know that. Tell us what's been going on."

They strolled very slowly down toward the racecourse,
and Joe told them as well as he could.

"Who was the bloke who shut Ma Eaton up?" demanded
Terry, smiling fiercely.

"Some chap. I don't know. I hardly know any of 'em."
He looked at Mike. "Hadn't we better tell Mrs. Hoddell?"

"If only you wouldn't race around *doing* things," said

Mike, but he said it in a friendly, teasing way. "You said yourself you don't know whether to tell her or not, so why tell her? Everybody can't know everything *all* the time. This is one of the times when we don't know."

"*Someone's* going to tell her for sure, and then what?"

"Then we'll have to tell her the whole lot. She won't blame us for not knowing what to do. Only it mightn't happen. Don't you remember," Mike went on, "that time Tubby Edwards was knocking off all cash from telephone booths? Everyone was talking about it, at school and everywhere, for weeks, but Mrs. Edwards never knew till the police showed up at the house."

Terry nodded. "And when old Cockburn was going broke, he just kept on telling people he was selling out. They all let on they believed him."

Matt added, "And when everyone thought Mrs. Whitlock was dying of cancer, nobody told *her* about it."

Joe stood still, torn by doubts. "Only maybe Mrs. Hoddell *ought* to know. She might be able to make Andy see that he *doesn't* own Beecham Park."

"Maybe," said Mike. "We don't know, do we? Only— do you think *anyone* could make Andy believe that?"

Joe gave a tired sigh. "I don't think anyone could," he confessed. "Andy just knows he does. Can't blame him, the way everyone's going on."

"Of course you can't blame him. What would you think if you were Andy?"

They stood on the pavement, watching the busy turnstiles of Beecham Park. After a minute Mike said, "There's another thing, though—it's doing Andy a lot of good. He's twice as good as he was. Even if it crashes, he might still be better than he was. . . . Only I don't think it will crash. It's too strong."

Joe would have argued about this, for it seemed impossible that Andy's dream shouldn't come crashing about his ears sooner or later; but his eyes had just fallen on Charlie and Greg Willis, Ted Chance, and two other boys standing in a group outside one of the turnstiles. At that moment Andy himself came through the turnstiles carrying two large bags of potato chips. He tore open one bag and poured chips into the outstretched hands of the five boys.

"That's all," he told them. "You clear off now. Can't have half the kids of Appington Hill coming in without their parents are with them."

"Go on," said the man on the turnstile. "You heard the boss. Clear off, now." The five boys drifted away.

Andy suddenly saw his friends standing and watching him, all four of them together. His face lit up.

"Hey, Joe—hey, Mike! You want to come in? Coming Matt? You want to see the horses, Terry?"

"Not tonight, boy," said Mike gravely. "Too many of us."

"Thanks all the same, mate," added Joe.

Andy looked a little disappointed but nodded seriously. Mike pointed to the potato chips.

"Two bags? I thought the rent was one bag."

"There's two stalls." Andy explained. "I told the chap on the other one, too."

Mike looked at Joe.

"You win," said Joe helplessly. "He does own it."

10 Joe's Birthday

Since Andy's friends had at last decided there was nothing they could do about him, life became more normal than it had been for weeks. Andy was deeply satisfied to find that the quarrel was over and followed them about for a while in the old way. He was with them on Monday afternoon after school when Joe said, "Who's coming up to the lights? I want to see if Blessings have got any balsa."

"Balsa?" said Mike keenly as they headed up Wattle Road toward the traffic lights. "What's that for?"

"Model plane," said Joe. "It's my birthday on Saturday, and I think I'm getting the motor. We could make the plane in your workshop by then."

"Got a pattern?" asked Terry.

"Not yet. If Blessings have the balsa, they're pretty sure to have a pattern."

"A plane's a good idea," said Matt with enthusiasm. "Plenty of room in the park for flying."

Andy's eager voice came from behind them. "Will it fly, Joe? Hey, Joe! Will your plane fly?"

"I hope so," said Joe over his shoulder. After a minute Andy called again.

"Gee, Joe, I'm glad about your birthday."

"Thanks, boy."

At the traffic lights they waited for the green WALK sign and crossed. Blessings, the news agents on the corner, was full of people buying evening papers. Mike, Joe, Terry, and Matt went to the toy shelves to hunt for balsa and patterns. Andy stayed outside the shop and waited. Once he would simply have stared at the shop windows until the others came out, but lately he had lost the habit of waiting about. Instead, he wandered around the corner, past the windows of other shops in the next street, until he reached a narrow alley that led past a row of back doors. These were the back doors of the shops in Wattle Road. Andy looked down the alley at garbage cans and boxes of rubbish that the shops had put out. Some distance along was a splash of bright color, a large carton piled high with threads and tangles of color. Andy went into the alley to see what the brightness was.

The carton was full of paper streamers. Some had been used and were stuffed loosely into the box, making the heap of color that had caught Andy's eye; but underneath there were others, still in their tight rolls. The rolls were faded and dusty on the outside, old stock that couldn't be sold; but when Andy unrolled a foot or so from one of them, the bright, watery green inside was as gay as it could have been. There were blue, red, purple, some pink and orange, and a few of tarnished tinsel. Andy unrolled a little from this one and a little from that. The gay colors fluttered and curled about his fingers, teasing and exciting. They looked like Christmas and birthdays.

Andy forgot about his friends and the model plane. He

couldn't leave the streamers in the alley to be thrown away, but the carton was too heavy to lift. He found a smaller box on one of the heaps of rubbish and filled it with rolls of color. He started to carry it home, but in a little while his feet changed direction and turned toward Beecham Park. Christmas and birthdays. Joe's birthday. On Saturday, when the trotters were running.

Boxful by boxful, Andy took the streamers to Beecham Park and hid them behind the old stand. On the second trip he passed Bert Hammond watering the garden.

"Nice day," said Bert. "Doing a bit of work over there?"

Andy nodded and chuckled, spikes of hair making a crest on the back of his head. "Surprise," he said mysteriously.

He brought some more streamers down the next afternoon, but after that the big carton vanished from the alley. It didn't really matter, for by then it was almost empty. Andy wandered about the racecourse wondering what to do with a great pile of colored streamers.

"There'll be something," he thought comfortably. "It's not till Saturday." He went off to the workshop in O'Days' back yard.

Mike was delicately cutting out shapes traced on a sheet of balsa wood while Matt watched him, absorbed. Terry and Joe were gluing pieces together, Joe holding the glued pieces carefully while Terry arranged tins, boxes, and books to keep them in position while they set. Andy slid quietly past them and crouched against the wall to watch.

"Hey, Joe, I bet you wish it was Saturday. . . . Don't you wish it was Saturday, Joe?"

"Yeah," said Joe, holding the tail assembly of the plane as if it might explode.

"Watch that glue," said Mike. "It's got to balance."

"It's gotta hold, too," grunted Terry.

"I bet you get a surprise on your birthday, Joe. I got something to show you on your birthday, down at my race-course. . . . You gotta come down and see, Joe. It's special."

Absorbed in the model plane, the boys hardly heard him at first, but Andy was not discouraged. For the next few days he returned to his theme whenever he saw Joe. Joe would frown in a puzzled way, while Mike looked on in silence and Terry and Matt with curiosity.

"You going?" asked Terry softly on Friday afternoon.

"I wish he'd give up," said Joe crossly. "I don't know what he's got in his head."

"All of you can come," said Andy kindly, "only Joe's gotta." He chuckled with excitement.

On Saturday afternoon, while the others were trickling fuel into the new motor of Joe's plane and trying it out, Andy was not there. He was, in fact, perched on the roof of the old stand at Beecham Park, having decided at last to use his streamers on the place that seemed to need them most. There was also the fact the streamers were there, right behind the stand. The ground was highest at this point. He had only to hoist a boxful of streamers to the top of a fencepost, climb up on the roof, and lift the box across.

The beams that supported the iron roof rested on a bearer across the open front of the stand, and the bearer rested on supporting posts. By lying on the flat, sloping roof, Andy could easily reach the beams at the sides and the bearer in front. He began to festoon his streamers across the front of the stand, unrolling them as he went, looping and twisting them around the bearer or the ends of the beams. One streamer didn't go very far, but it didn't matter because there were such a lot of them. Sometimes he would tie an end around one of the upright posts; and once, when he was doing this, he dropped the whole roll to the ground. At first he tried to haul it up, but of course it simply unwound as he pulled.

"Doesn't matter," he told himself. "It can go round the post." After a while he went back over his tracks and tied more streamers to the posts, dropping the rolls to the ground.

At first the streamers hung in sparse, untidy garlands between the electric lamps on the front of the stand. Then they grew into thick festoons of tangled color—red, blue, mauve, green, and orange, with a touch of tinsel here and there. Andy chuckled with excitement and delight as he fetched another boxful. He was too intent to notice the man in overalls who paused and stared, running his fingers through his hair.

After a time there were several men gazing up at the stand, grinning or looking uncertain.

"Well, I dunno . . ."

"Not doing any harm that *I* can see."

"Brightening up the old Leger. That'll make 'em think."

"What about the blokes cleaning up tomorrow?"

"I'm one. They won't mind."

"Well, I dunno . . ."

"I want to see Marsden's face when he spots this lot." The grins widened.

"Do you think Bert Hammond's going to let it go that far? Not a chance, mate."

"Yeah? I reckon we can handle Bert."

When Andy had used up all the streamers, he climbed down and admired his work from the ground. He collected the rolls he had dropped from above and wound those

streamers around and around the posts, tying them at the bottom. The men came wandering by, one by one, calling friendly greetings.

"Brightening her up a bit, boss?"

"That's a bit of all right. They'll think it's Christmas."

Andy would pause and give them his shy, direct smile. "It's Joe's birthday. He's my friend."

"That so? Friend's birthday, eh? He'll get a surprise, then."

Andy never saw Bert Hammond come striding across, for Bert ran into a solid wall of men who closed him around. Neither did Andy hear the scraps of talk that drifted his way, for his mind was fixed on the work his hands were doing.

". . . can't see the harm in it . . . not getting in anyone's way . . ." And then, more strongly, "You just tell 'em if they don't like it, they can start looking for someone else to put on the gates tonight, and do the cleaning in the morning, too." Finally, in a voice that held something like scorn, "They'll never notice, Bert. They don't care what goes on in the Leger."

Andy, with a last excited chuckle, walked straight past the group of men and went home for his dinner. Bert went off more nervously to wait for the secretary of the Committee.

That evening Andy burst into O'Days' back yard before the first car of the evening had been trapped and set the yard throbbing with his eager impatience. "Are you coming down, Joe? Hey, Joe? You'll get a surprise if you do. Aren't you coming, Joe?"

"You'll have to tell him," whispered Mike. "He'll burst if you don't."

"Oh, *all right!*" cried Joe at last. "Put a sock in it, can't you, Andy? I'll come." It was not really Andy's insistence that exasperated him. It was because he knew he really had no choice—he couldn't hurt Andy by refusing.

"Good on you, Joe!" cried Andy, hugging himself. "I bet you'll be glad. You coming, too, Mike? Eh, Matt? Eh, Terry?"

In the end, of course, they all went, feeling guilty but full of curiosity about Andy's surprise.

"I bet he's giving you this week's rent," whispered Matt. It seemed to all of them the most likely surprise.

The man on the turnstile was a little startled to see so many of them, but he let them all through. Matt and Terry, not having been inside before, stared at the crowd, at the great floating grandstand, and at the dark, rippling pool inside the track. Andy led them straight to the small stand.

It was even better than he remembered. Now the strings of lights had been switched on. They glowed among the tangled streamers that stirred and rustled in the breeze, lighting the colors to brilliance and throwing on the ground shadows that moved a little like snakes. The shabby old stand seemed to be dressed up for a play. People were staring at it and chattering in a lively way. Andy's blue eyes were round and shining. He was almost as astonished as the people.

"I forgot!" he said. "I never thought of the lights. Gee, it's good, isn't it? Are you glad, Joe? I did it for your birthday. See, I *said* I had a surprise. Do you like it, Joe?"

"Andy! You didn't do that?"

"I did, though. Found 'em at the back of Blessings—put out for the garbage, they were. Good, aren't they?"

Joe's face was red and embarrassed, Terry's and Matt's blank with shock, but Mike was grinning. A voice in the crowd said, "*There's* the owner. How you going, boss?"

"Honest now, Andy," said Mike, "did you do it off your own bat?"

"I said already. For Joe's birthday. Aren't you glad, Joe?"

Joe wore a hunted expression, but he made an effort and said, "Gee, Andy, I never had a surprise like that. Thanks, boy. Let's—let's get a bit further away—where we can see it better."

Across the lighted circle of the track and on the other side of the course, an expensively dressed gentleman in a bowler hat was speaking to another. "What's going on in the Leger tonight, Marsden? I don't think very highly of that stand—who's responsible for it?"

The secretary of the Committee shifted unhappily. "I understand the men are celebrating something. Hammond reports that they threatened to walk off if it was interfered with. It seemed wiser not to create a disturbance when the gates were due to open in half an hour."

The expensive gentleman frowned, staring across the course at the tangled colors that glowed and shifted between the lights. "The men took a bit of a liberty, it seems to me. If we get complaints from patrons on that side, the Committee will want to hear more about it."

On their side of the course, Andy's friends waited with

him to see one race and to collect his rent from the two stalls, but Mike and Joe were uneasy in case their parents should hear of this adventure. It wasn't safe to be here with Andy. There were too many smiles, too many cheerful remarks about the decorations, too many good-natured voices following them.

"Stand back, mate—let the owner through."

"There you are, boss. Big gala night tonight, eh?"

The trouble was, thought Joe, that most of these people *wanted* Andy to be the owner. As soon as he could, he said, "Well, thanks, boy, that was great. Only I better get home now or there'll be a row."

Andy dealt out potato chips from one of his bags. "I better get home myself, even. Have to be down early tomorrow and clean up those streamers."

They trudged up Blunt Street, crunching potato chips as they went. When Andy went loping away down his own street, Matt sighed deeply and spoke his first words since entering Beecham Park.

"I never saw anything like that. That's—that's—well, I know what Mike means for once. He owns the place. He does."

Terry said sourly, "At two bags of chips a week, he'll even make a profit in the end. If it goes on long enough."

11 Strange Characters

Andy went down to the racecourse early the next morning and began to take down the streamers. He was pulling down those that were twisted around the upright posts when the cleaners began to arrive. They shouted cheerfully to him and each other.

"What did I tell you? Cleaning up his own mess, see?"

"How did your friend like his birthday surprise, boss?"

George, the small man with lively brown eyes, insisted on climbing to the roof himself to tear down the streamers from above.

"You don't want to bother," said Andy. "I put 'em up, didn't I?"

"That's all right, mate—can't have the owner breaking his neck. You don't want to keep a dog and bark yourself. I'll just drop the lot down, and you can shove it in the bins."

So George went up a ladder and threw down armfuls of colored paper quicker than Andy could gather them up. Sometimes he would aim them at Andy so that he was draped in coils of orange, purple, and green. Andy would laugh until he almost fell down, and the other men would pause in their work and grin. The job was soon done, and Andy and George helped with the sweeping in the ordinary way.

Not only here, but outside the walls of Beecham Park, people seemed to have enjoyed Joe's birthday surprise. Wherever Andy went, they would speak to him about it in much the same way as the sweepers had. He began to see that the whole thing was more important than he had thought and even rather clever.

"That brightened her up, that did," said Andy proudly, swaggering down Wattle Road with his hands in his pockets. Then he frowned heavily, trying to think of some other important, exciting thing that an owner could do with a racecourse.

Ahead of him, four figures that he knew well turned from Blunt Street into Wattle Road and walked down toward the park. Andy hurried to catch up with them. Joe's model plane, fully assembled and already past its first test flight, was about to be tested again.

To Andy, the flying of the plane was a small and perfect miracle. He followed, watched, and listened, so quiet that his friends hardly knew he was there. He never once called to them, never once laughed or chuckled. He only watched, listened, and followed.

"We'll have to keep her out of the way of that kite. Through the arches—there'll be more room there."

Andy went with them through one wide arch of the railway crossing to the broad, sunny stretch beyond.

"Down here away from the trees. Look out, you're spilling the fuel."

Andy sniffed the smell of ether and heard the fierce little engine sputter and whine.

"Tail's right this time. That wing needs a bit more weight."

"It's not the wing. The engine's not dead even. I told you that."

"Well, we're not going to take it out again unless we have to, are we? Put a bit more weight on the wing."

Andy listened and watched the little plane fly free and brave above the railway arches. Not until the sun had gone and they were walking home did he speak, and then he called softly from behind.

"Joe! Hey, Joe . . . you're the owner, aren't you?"

It was still early when he reached home, so he wandered out to the laundry to rummage in the cupboard under the tubs. There were no tools like those in O'Days' workshop, but he found a set of small wrenches, an old rusted tin of paint, and a paintbrush with short, scraggy bristles. He took them inside to ask his mother if he might have them.

"That old stuff?" said his mother. "I shouldn't think it's much good for anything. What do you want it for?"

Andy's eyes went vacant, and his mouth dropped open a little. His mother gave a tiny sigh.

"Something the boys are making, is it? I had an idea you weren't seeing so much of the boys lately. You haven't had a row with them, have you, love?"

"Mike and Joe had a row," said Andy, frowning. Then he chuckled. "They made it up now."

"Oh, was *that* it? Well, at least it's soon made up. Take that old stuff if you want it, but don't make a mess for Mrs. O'Day."

Andy took his things out to the back yard and managed to pry the lid off the tin with one of the wrenches. There was a thick, wrinkled coat on top of the paint and under that a lot of yellow oil. He lifted off the scum with a stick and tried to stir it. It was very thick and heavy, but the stick came out fresh and white. He remembered the white rails at Beecham Park and the white benches for the band to sit on. He kept on stirring the paint till his hand was tired, then tipped the rest of the oil gently off. He was chuckling, thinking how pleased the men would be if he gave those benches a fresh coat of paint. He remembered helping his mother to paint the kitchen table once. You had to give it time to dry. They hadn't been able to use the table for a day and a night.

He kept the little wrenches in his pocket, where they jingled now and then as he moved. It was nearly as good as having a workshop, like the O'Day boys who could build planes. He took the paint and brush down to Beecham Park on Wednesday afternoon when the gates were locked, so that no one should see him at work. He wanted his painting to be a surprise for everyone, like the streamers. With the brush and tin stuffed into the front of his shirt, he climbed over the gate. The wrenches jingled as he jumped down.

The big grandstand loomed over him, empty and stern. He had to dodge under the rails and cross the track to reach the benches. There were three of them. Their white paint was yellowed and stained with patches of rust and black. Andy frowned importantly at them and went to work. He did the job as quickly as he could, simply pouring the thick paint out of the tin and spreading it with his stubby brush.

When it was finished, he stood back and looked at it proudly.

"That's wet paint, that is," he said, and went hunting for something to make a sign.

He found an old sheet of cardboard against the fence behind one of the buildings and, screwing up his face intently, scrawled WET PAINT on it with his brush. He propped it near the benches, dropped the brush and paint tin into a garbage bin, and climbed back over the gate.

By now it was growing dusk, and just as Andy reached the ground, a voice spoke out of the dusk and made him jump.

"What's a young feller like you doing in this place of wickedness?" said the voice. It was hollow and accusing.

"Eh?" said Andy, staring.

A thin, angry-looking man was gazing darkly back at him, leaning against the wall. "Haven't you got nowhere better to go, boy?" he demanded sternly. "This here's no place for you. The abode of evil, that's what it is. You want to keep away from it."

Andy laughed. "You're wrong there, mister. This is Beecham Park racecourse, this is. I thought everyone knew that."

The thin man leaned forward, so that his pale face hung over Andy in the dusk. He was frowning. "You take notice of your elders that's sent to guide you, boy. This is the abode of evil, all right, and a snare for your innocent young feet. This is where the wicked man flourishes with his lies and deceits, taking the bread out of the children's mouths so that he can ride around in his big car, all black and shiny.

You don't want to let him catch you. You keep away from here."

Andy was troubled. "I never seen him, mister. I got a lot of good friends here. Are you sure you got the right place?" He could tell from the pale, stern face that the man was sure, so he went on quickly. "I'll watch out for that feller with the big black car. If I see him, I'll set Bert Hammond on him. *He'll* fix him."

This promise did not seem to calm the angry man. "I've warned you, young feller," he began. Andy could see there was only one way to end the argument, so he took it at once.

"I got to go, mister," he said, and loped heavily away. A black dog with a hairless, leathery back came sniffing after him, and Andy clicked his fingers at it.

"I never seen that chap, the one that takes bread away from kids," he told the dog. "That other old bloke, he's got it mixed up somehow. Some other racecourse, that's what it is."

Still, he meant to keep an eye open, but by next afternoon, when he strolled down in search of Bert Hammond, he had forgotten. He went through the open gate with only a secret glance and chuckle at the white benches with their warning sign. He had a sort of hope that no one would notice the fresh paint until Saturday night—and that then they would all notice and be astonished.

In fact, several people had noticed the benches already, but no one had inspected them closely. Drivers taking trotters around the course for training had seen the white paint as they saw everything about the track, but a patch of white had no importance to horses used to the movement and color and lights of race nights. Marsden, the secretary of the Committee had noticed with slight irritation, because it seemed to him that old Hammond was using paint and time without authority; but the secretary was more concerned about last Saturday night and whether the Committee would want to hear more about it. Why the men should suddenly want to hang streamers on the old stand and threaten to go on strike about it was more than he could explain. Time enough to worry about the unauthorized use of paint when someone asked to be paid for it. Bert Hammond had also noticed the paint with irritation, but Bert, too, had other things to worry about. If Marsden wanted to pay someone else to do work that Bert could have done in his ordinary time, why should Bert worry? He went on watering the garden while he thought about Andy and the men.

"Made a sort of mascot of him," muttered Bert, and wondered what he ought to do if the whole thing was going to get out of hand—until he found himself looking at the open, friendly face, the round blue eyes, and the spikes of hair of Andy himself.

"The onion weed's dead," said Andy, jingling the wrenches in his pocket. "Will it grow again, Mr. Hammond?"

"Sure as fate," said Bert gloomily.

Andy was surprised. "Don't you like onion weed, Mr. Hammond?"

"It's not the *onion weed* bothering me," said Bert. "No harm in a bit of weed."

"Good," said Andy simply, and began to pull out other,

less favored weeds. Bert watched him, frowning, while he searched for the right words. At last he spoke.

"I reckon you're too young to own a racecourse after all."

Andy chuckled. Then he saw how sternly Bert was frowning. His eyes slid away, and he made clumsy, defiant snatches at the weeds. "I got one already," he muttered. "That's nothing, about being too young."

Bert was brutal. "I reckon it's something. I reckon you're a lot too young. You can't look after a racecourse."

Andy turned on him stormily, eyebrows drawn down, for he had never expected to be attacked by Bert Hammond. "You shut up!" he raged. "*You* don't own it! You ask anyone. *They'll* tell you if I'm the owner."

This was only too true, and while Bert looked for an answer, Andy's rage faded. "See, I bought it," he insisted in a hurt, lost voice.

Bert's face softened in spite of himself. "That's not enough, just buying it," he said. "Nobody owns a racecourse all by himself. Nobody owns much all by himself, and that's a fact. You take a racecourse—what's the good of it without the trainers bringing their dogs and horses? And the people paying to come and watch? You got to look after it right, or they won't come—and then what have you got? A bit of land, maybe, and a few old buildings, but you haven't got a racecourse."

"They come, don't they? Gee, a whole lot of them come every time!"

"You go fooling around with colored streamers, turning the place into a toyshop, and they won't. They'll soon get tired of that. A racecourse isn't meant to be a toyshop."

"Those streamers, they *liked* 'em. Everyone liked 'em; you ask anyone."

"In the Leger they might have thought it was a joke, but they didn't like it in the stand. The Committee didn't like it."

Andy bent over the weeds, yanking them out vigorously. "You can't tell," he muttered. "That's what it is."

"Of course you can't," Bert agreed heartily. "You got to be at it for years, like me. You come and ask me, every single time, and I'll put you right." After all, he thought, it was the men who caused the trouble. No use blaming the kid.

Andy thought uneasily of the band's seats, but it was too late to ask Bert about those now. Besides, he was still bitterly hurt by Bert's attack when everyone else had been so pleased with the streamers. He stood up and wandered off by himself along the rails, muttering resentfully. "*He's* not the owner. He needn't go for *me*." He walked on, inspecting the rails closely, examining the way they were bolted to their uprights, trying the wrenches on the nuts to see if they would fit. One wrench fitted. He tugged at it, tightening nuts that were already tight.

"What are you doing *now?*" shouted Bert nervously. He was winding up the hose and keeping an eye on Andy.

"Nothing," shouted Andy, tugging at another nut.

"That can't hurt," muttered Bert. Muttering to himself, Andy dodged under the rail and across the track, out of sight.

Beyond the inner rail lay the grass track where the greyhounds ran, and here were the rails along which, like a train on its lines, ran the bogey that drew the mechanical hare. There were nuts here too, and Andy tugged at one or two. Suddenly he was tired of being here, angry and hurt. He went back through the rails and started to go home.

He looked at the benches as he passed. "That'll be all right," he muttered. "Those seats, they were white before." Then he paused in the gateway, shoulders humped and hands in pockets, jingling his wrenches. Bert Hammond was putting the rolled-up hose away in a shed. Andy went loping quickly to the benches.

The fresh paint stared at him accusingly. It had wrinkled a little here and there, but he touched it with his finger, and it felt quite dry. Stealthily, he crushed the cardboard sign into a small, crumpled bundle and slipped away with it, out of the gate.

He didn't go back to Beecham Park until Saturday night, for he was truly offended with Bert. Instead, he spent his spare time watching his friends fly Joe's model plane. He was fascinated by the plane, so alive and tricky, attacking the air so fiercely and coming down so dangerously; but on Saturday night, when the drone of bigger motors sounded in the street and the giant voice from Beecham Park spoke into the room, he remembered Bert Hammond frowning at him and the band's seats. He slipped quietly away, going by the alley and the vacant ground where the stray cats lived.

There were two men there, standing near the stairs in the glow of the sunset and gazing down at the walls and gateways of the racecourse. Andy tried to pass quietly behind them, but they must have heard him. They swung around.

"Here's the kid," said one of them sharply. Then he spoke
to Andy in a hearty, friendly voice. "Here's the owner himself. You *are* the owner, aren't you, mate?"

"That's me," said Andy, shuffling his feet. The two sharp
faces, smiling so widely, made him feel uncomfortable, but
they were standing between him and the stairs. "I gotta go
now," he said tentatively, but the men didn't move.

"Fancy that, now, Tom," said one of them to the other.
"The owner himself, a young chap like this. Of course I'd
heard about it, but I'd never have believed it, would you?"

"Not me," said Tom. "Going down to keep an eye on
the place, are you, mate?" Andy shuffled his feet again.

The first man laughed. "Of course he is, Tom; he has to!
Can't run a place like this without keeping an eye on it.
Grounds, track, kennels, stables, feedstalls—he's into everything, this young chap. That's right, son?" When Andy
only stared at him, he repeated the question sharply. "Go
where you like down there, don't you?"

"I can if I like," said Andy. He didn't like these two smiling men.

"I bet you can. Know all the horses, too, I bet. Now I
wonder if you know Fair Lady? I've got a special interest in
her—known her since a filly—friend of her owner."

Andy did know Fair Lady. "Reg Watson drives her," he
said.

"That's right, that's her. My word, you might be able to
do me a little favor if you've got a minute to spare. I'm in a
bit of a rush myself. Got to go off to the country, so I'm
just a bit squeezed for time. Now, I always go and see Fair

Lady before a race and take her a little snack—aniseed, that's what she likes, mixed in a bit of mash. Well, being a bit rushed tonight, I just can't make it, and I'm afraid it might put her off her race if she doesn't get aniseed. She looks forward to it, see? Well, I know a lot of people wouldn't

worry about a thing like that, but that's not me. I do worry. Wouldn't be fair if she lost her race on my account, would it? Now, if you could take it down for me—I've got it here —and just put it in her feedstall—would you do that?" The man held out a small package.

Andy stared at it. "I dunno," he said.

"Well, of course," said the man, smiling still more widely, "I wouldn't expect an important bloke like you to waste your valuable time for *nothing*. I'd have to make *that* up to you, wouldn't I? Two dollars? Is that fair?" Andy was astonished to see a note in the man's other hand and to find package and note thrust firmly into his own hands. He went on staring. "It's worth that to me," the man was saying, "if it's worth it to you, to see that the little mare gets a fair chance. Only I wouldn't mention it to anyone if I were you. There's those that might like to see her lose. Good night to you. We'll get on our way."

The two men hurried down the stairs and into a car that was waiting in the street below. Though they were in such a hurry, the car didn't drive off at once. Andy saw that it was black and shining. Then he knew who the men must be.

"The evil fellers!" he muttered. "Those ones that take bread from kids!" He went loping down the stairs, past the colored lights of the hotel, and across the street to the open gate of the racecourse.

The grandstand rose before him, dressed in its lights. The band was playing, the same mixed lot in their dark blue uniforms with various trimmings, marching forward along the track. The crowd on the rails craned after them, listening and staring. Andy had no time to listen. He turned his eyes away from the lights to the shadows by the gate, looking for the tall, quiet form of Bert Hammond.

Bert was there. Andy thrust the package and the two-dollar note at him urgently. "Two fellers gave me this for Fair Lady. They're in a big black car. What'll I do?"

"Where's the car?" snapped Bert.

"That one—see, it's turning around—it's going up the hill. Are they bad men, Mr. Hammond?"

"Got the number," said Bert with satisfaction, fishing with his free hand for a pencil and scribbling on the package that was meant for Fair Lady. Then he looked at Andy, and his square mouth stretched into a smile. "Bad men, all right. You know what, son? You'll make a pretty good owner after all, I shouldn't wonder. You did the right thing that time."

Warm little trickles of relief and pleasure flowed through Andy's body. He chuckled happily and stared at the track. Then—his mouth fell open in frozen horror.

The band had turned and was marching away down the track, swinging proudly to the rhythm of their own music while their instruments shone under the floodlights: two very short men, two very old men, some with red stripes and some with gold braid; but all with patches of white paint and strips of wrinkled scum clinging to the seats of their navy-blue trousers.

Andy turned and went running away.

12 The Hare Wins a Race

"You understand, I had to tell 'em," said Bert Hammond, his jaw square and stern. "The row—I never saw such a to-do. Talk of the police, and all." He pressed a hand against his forehead. "I told Marsden the whole thing—couldn't do different."

He was talking, not to Andy, but to Andy's four friends. Andy himself was sunk in shame and misery and had taken to haunting lonely lanes and avoiding people's eyes. His friends had found him that dreadful night running down a dark street and moaning softly to himself. Full of alarm, they ran after him.

"Andy! Andy, old boy, what's up? Come on, boy, tell us what it is."

"The band," moaned Andy. "Their pants—the paint— I done it. Gee, I should've asked Bert."

They got the story out of him bit by bit, and none of them felt like laughing. They were horrified, but they had to try to comfort Andy.

"Never mind, old boy; don't you worry. A bit of paint? Dry-cleaning'll take that off."

They even tried to make a joke of it, though they knew

it was really a crisis. The white paint on the band's trousers was a sort of earthquake rocking Andy's frail castle. They could see that he wasn't worried about this, but they couldn't make him laugh either. He was simply horrified at what he had done to the band. They kept him with them in the workshop for over two hours, and when he was calmer, they took him home.

He didn't help with the sweeping in the morning but crept miserably to Bert Hammond's front gate and waited until Bert came out. "Gee, I'm sorry, Mr. Hammond," he whispered. "Gee, I never meant it to be like that. I'll always ask you after this, so you can put me straight."

"You mightn't have much chance, son," said Bert, trying to warn him for his own sake. "I'll do my best for you, but the Committee won't be pleased. There'll be a row."

"Will I have to buy new pants with stripes on 'em? I got no money, see."

"You can't buy 'em, then, can you? I reckon the Committee'll look after that side of it."

"They're the ones that get the money," said Andy, working it out. "That's fair, I reckon."

"The Committee won't think it's very fair," said Bert sharply. "I got to warn you, boy; there'll be a row. It wasn't the Committee that smothered those benches with old paint."

"Gee, I know that, Mr. Hammond. Not *their* fault those seats was all black and rusty. *I'm* the owner; I got to look after them." This point of view silenced Bert for a moment. Andy whispered, "But I never meant—the band—the pants . . ." He slunk quickly away.

Bert was not really surprised that his warning had failed

to get through. He was worried about Andy and glad to see
Andy's four friends when they came to ask, rather nervously, what was likely to happen.

"You understand, I had no choice but to tell 'em," he said.
"The Committee's meeting tomorrow night. They'll have
the whole story from Marsden."

The boys were silent for a moment, awed by the thought
of a number of expensively dressed gentlemen in bowler
hats sitting around a table and discussing Andy Hoddell,
the rival owner of their racecourse. Mike said, "Where do
they meet?"

"Committee room down there," said Bert absently, waving toward the grandstand at Beecham Park. "Poor kid. . . .
I blame the men for leading him on, but it's mostly my fault.
. . . Still and all, there wasn't much anyone could do. He's
got this idea so firm in his head you can't get it out, and you
don't know the harm you might do trying."

"We know," agreed Joe heartily. "Well—if only his
mother doesn't have to hear, that's the best we can look for
now."

"I'll do my best for him," Bert promised. "That business
with Fair Lady ought to help." He told them about it.
"Saved a bit of a rumpus, that did; they can't help but be
pleased about that. I'll do my best with it." His eyes slid
away, looking downhill and across the racecourse. "I've
been with it for a long time . . ."

The boys crept away. They were shaken to realize that
other people—Bert Hammond, the men who worked in
the grounds, Marsden the secretary—were being drawn
into Andy's troubles. They were glad that Bert was going

to do his best, and secretly, unreasonably, they were full of a new hope.

"Those crooks that were trying to dope the horse," said Terry tensely, "I bet that makes a big difference!"

Matt's eyes danced. "He said so himself—it can't help but make a difference! My sainted aunt—fancy old Andy nabbing them!"

"All the same," said Joe, looking sideways at Mike, "you were wrong. He doesn't really own the place. If he did, we wouldn't be wondering what's going to happen. It *couldn't* crash."

"Couldn't it?" retorted Mike. "We used to have a big garden in front of our place, but they took it off us to make the street wider. There's my uncle, too. He's a tanner, and they made him shift his business because people didn't like the smell. He owned his yard and sheds all right, but they made him shift out, all the same."

Terry curled his lip. "You mean Andy owns Beecham Park but not the band's trousers."

Matt gave a snort of laughter. Suddenly, they were all leaning against the wall and laughing till it hurt.

"I wish I'd seen them!"

"Poor old Andy!"

"Marching along—*oomp-ah, oomp-ah* . . ."

". . . and all that white paint on their pants!"

They were still there, leaning weakly against the wall, when Andy found them. They took him up to the traffic lights to buy him a drink. He followed quietly, but they thought he seemed less miserable than he had been; and once they heard his voice from behind.

"It'll be right. Dry-cleaning'll take that off."

Matt choked a little.

As they reached the busier streets, they began to realize that other people were laughing, too.

"How are you, boss? Doing any more painting?" said a man outside Blessings.

"Don't worry mate; we'll stand up for you," called the men outside the hotel.

Andy turned pink and chuckled faintly.

The next evening, with Andy safely at home, the others wandered out restlessly to look at Beecham Park where the Committee was meeting. There were one or two cars in the grounds, and a dim light shone from a room under the big stand.

"We can get around to the back of that," said Mike.

They went down to the park and worked quietly around the lower wall of the racecourse until they found an open gate. They slipped through it and along one side of the stand where another lighted window was partly open. They sat in a silent row underneath it, leaning against the wall. A rumble of men's voices came through the window.

"No good," whispered Joe. "Can't hear."

They would have left, but a late-coming car kept them frozen while the beam of its headlights fumbled past them and reached across the grounds. By the time the driver had disappeared through a door in the front of the stand, an outbreak of louder voices was coming through the window. The boys sat and listened to the phrases they could hear.

". . . find it very difficult to believe . . ."

"Never heard such nonsense!"

"Disgraceful lack of control . . . not the Committee's responsibility."

Someone banged with something, and a single voice spoke quietly on; but tempers seemed to be rising in the room, and it was not long before loud voices broke out again.

"Ridiculous story!"

"We shall be a laughing-stock!"

"Public opinion . . . very strong feelings among the men . . . nasty incident avoided . . . Fair Lady . . ."

Then one voice, very loud: "Are you suggesting that this Committee should be held to *ransom?*"

More banging and a call: "Gentlemen! Gentlemen! Difficult matter . . . undesirable publicity . . . further consideration . . ."

There was silence for a moment and then a general rumbling of voices. Mike tugged at the sleeve nearest him. "I think they're coming out," he whispered.

The four listeners drifted quietly off to the park, where they paused and looked at each other rather wildly.

"But what did they *decide?*" cried Matt. "As far as I can see, they just gave up and went home."

"They've got to find a way to keep it dark," said Terry. "They don't want a row with the men and stories in the papers and all that."

"That's something," said Joe moodily. "No more do we."

They walked home in silence; and as they separated Mike said, "They've still got to find a way to make Andy *believe* he isn't the owner. They haven't even started yet." Then he grinned. "Rocked them a bit, didn't it?—finding out that someone else owned their racecourse."

It did seem that the Committee's meeting had made very little difference. The incident of the band's trousers began to fade in importance, even to Andy's friends. Andy himself was recovering rapidly. "I made a mistake, see," he said to Joe. "I got to be in it for years yet. Then I'll know." On the day after that, he invited his friends to come down and watch the greyhounds training, just as if nothing had happened.

"I'd rather watch from the top of the cliff," said Joe quickly. "You can see more from up there."

They went to the cliff and sat on the rocks. Men and dogs moved about below as casually as they always did on a training night. It was early, and at first the mechanical hare was not moving; but in a moment the high mechanical whine came up to the cliff, and the small bobbing shape went swinging around the course, gathering speed as it approached the barrier where some of the dogs waited. As it swung past, the barrier doors opened, and three greyhounds sprang after it. The hare raced ahead, bobbing bravely—until suddenly it paused and seemed to consider. The whining sound increased, but the hare moved sedately, with teasing slowness, for a yard or two while the dogs hurled themselves at it. Then, with the sudden speed of a bullet, it shot away to the other side of the track while the dogs yelped with bewilderment. They had lost it. The hare dropped back to its normal racing speed while three men ran out on the track to collect the bewildered dogs.

Andy was laughing joyously. "Did you see him go? They lost him! He nearly caught 'em up from behind." He laughed and laughed.

Now again the hare came past the barrier, and four more dogs leaped after it. The hare swung ahead—and again, at the same spot, it paused, went slowly while the dogs caught up, then shot off at amazing speed halfway around the track. Then it stopped. Andy lay back against the rock and laughed helplessly.

"There's something wrong," said Mike, frowning.

"Notice how the whine goes up when she slows down?" said Terry. "They put on more power, trying to get her through the slow bit, and when she comes through, she's going like a rocket till they get her slowed down again. There's something wrong with the rail at that place where she slows down."

"Eh?" said Andy, still chuckling. "Not there, there isn't. I tightened those nuts myself. With my wrench I did it."

They were staring at him.

"*Andy!*"

"*Oh, no*—you didn't, did you?"

"What's up?" said Andy. He lay back and laughed again.

They carried him off to the workshop and there, in private, explained. By tightening those nuts, they said, he had forced together the rails along which ran the bogey that drew the hare; so that at that point, they said, the wheels of the bogey were squeezed too tightly by the rails and had to force their way through. They showed him, using the skateboard and two lengths of wood arranged as rails. There would be no more greyhound-training tonight, they explained gravely.

"Don't you worry; they'll fix it all right," Andy assured them. "I can show 'em which nuts."

"No!"

"No, you needn't do that!"

"They'll find the nuts, all right. But they won't be pleased."

Andy was sober for a moment. Then he remembered the hare, teasingly luring the dogs close only to shoot away; and he laughed and laughed. "I never did no harm this time," he said coaxingly. "Not like those trousers."

Finally, Matt took him home for the night while the others sat on in a tired way. This was the end, they knew. No matter how adverse the publicity, no matter if every man on the grounds went on strike, those angry Committee men would have no more of Andy. His dream castle was tottering. It would crash.

The very next afternoon, as they went down Wattle Road with Andy following, they saw Bert Hammond waiting at the corner. They hesitated, then went slowly forward. Bert put a hand on Andy's shoulder.

"Come along, son. Marsden wants a word with you."

"Eh?" said Andy, and Bert drew him on toward Beecham Park while the others watched.

"This is it," said Joe grimly; and they went slowly on to the gate themselves, watching the solid, rather clumsy figure of Andy going with Bert toward the farther end of the big stand, where it disappeared from sight. They waited by the gate, swinging their school bags and not speaking, for what seemed a long time.

"Here he comes," said Mike at last.

Andy was coming slowly back, pausing, looking about him, and coming on again. In the background, Bert stood and watched him go as his four friends were watching him come. Lost in thought and often stopping, Andy came on until he saw the group at the gate. Even then he didn't hurry, and they saw that his face was solemn and absorbed. As soon as he was close enough, he began to talk in a voice that was full of awe.

"You know what they did, Mike? Those ones that get the money—you know what they did, Joe? They bought Beecham Park. They bought it off me. Look." He opened one hand a little and showed them some crumpled notes. "Ten dollars, they paid me. That's a lot more than it cost me."

A little breath stirred the four boys at the gate. Andy looked from face to face and saw that they were impressed. "I had to sign a paper," he said importantly.

"You sold it to them, did you?" said Mike. He didn't know what else to say; but he sent his silent thanks across the racecourse to Bert Hammond, Marsden the secretary, and the Committee. Whether they had meant it like this or not, they had found a way for Andy.

"Three dollars," said Andy. "That's what they said first. They wanted to give me three dollars, like I paid the old bloke. I *had* three dollars before. I told 'em that. What do I want with three dollars when I got a racecourse already? I told 'em that."

Terry grinned. "What did they say then?"

"Oh—they talked a lot of stuff about a new stand they want—and those seats, what I did—and then they gave me *ten* dollars. That's a lot of money, *ten* dollars is. So now I got no racecourse."

"Never mind," said Joe quickly. "We'll go up on the cliff every Saturday night and watch, just the same. You made a good deal—what are you going to do with all that money?"

Andy gave a puzzled chuckle. "I dunno," he said, and followed his friends out of the gate and up the hill.

They spent the afternoon in the workshop fixing the O'Days' lawnmower. Andy sat in a corner and watched, clutching his notes. Just as he was leaving to go home, he paused in the doorway. "Hey, Joe! Could I have a plane like yours, Joe? Is this enough money?"

"We'll fix it for you," Mike promised. He was thinking rather sadly that soon they would all be used to an orderly, peaceful life in which Andy Hoddell no longer owned Beecham Park Trotting Course. When Andy had gone, Mike looked slyly at Joe.

"You were wrong. It didn't crash. You forgot that Andy wouldn't let it."

"Andy! He couldn't have stopped it. It was Bert Hammond and the racecourse lot."

"And why do you think they went to all that trouble? There was nothing else they could do! Andy *knew* he owned the place, so they just had to see it his way."

"Maybe. We can't tell. Can we make him a plane for eight dollars?"

Matt said, "I know a chap with a motor that he might sell cheap."

"Is it any use?" said Terry. "He'll only bust it."

"What does it matter?" demanded Mike almost roughly. "He's got to have things sometimes, even if he does bust them."

Andy was sitting on his favorite patch of ground, among the stray cats, and gazing at the quiet grounds of Beecham Park. He might have been thinking of sea gulls, perhaps, or of greyhounds; of strong, dark horses whirling satin-clad drivers under the spraying lights. He might have been thinking of quiet afternoons and friendly people.

A man came striding up the stairs with a newspaper under his arm.

"There you are, boss. Keeping an eye on your property?"

"She's not mine," said Andy. "I sold her, see."